The American Dream: Love, Lust, and Lies!!!

Words Matter Publishing
P.O. Box 531
Salem, Il 62881
www.wordsmatterpublishing.com

ISBN 13: 978-1-953912-05-3

Library of Congress Catalog Card Number: 2020919726

TABLE OF CONTENTS

INTRODUCTION

As you read this book, please imagine that you are at a local Performing Arts Centre. You have parked your vehicle. You have picked up your ticket from the box office. You have entered the auditorium. You have been given a playbill. You are seated by the usher. It's about thirty minutes until "showtime." You begin to read about the play and the performers. Anticipation builds as you wait for the lights to dim, the curtains to open, and the play to start. Certainly, you will not be on stage, but you will become a part of the production as the plot unravels and is revealed. Hopefully, that is what happens as you read this book. The story takes place in "Anytown, USA" and not in any particular period of time. It is up to you, the reader, to fill in those blanks. The main characters are Charles, Joann, Elizabeth, Edward, Butch and Beth. There are also many minor characters, too many to mention by name, that appear to have lesser roles and at the same time maybe have a major impact. All of the characters are intertwined and influence each other in some way. As you read the book and take the journey, pick out the role you are playing or would like to play. Then, decide how you will play the part. At the end of the book, compare your thoughts with the actions of the character you chose.

Chapter 1
CHARLES—THE RECURRING DREAMS

"Why do these nightmares keep happening?" I ask myself. "How do I make them go away?"

Another restless night and all because of these recurring dreams! As a child, I do not remember having that many dreams at night. I think it was because of all of the chores we had to do for our family to exist. Almost every night I went to bed extremely tired and was out of bed early the next morning. I do recall daydreaming in school, when my assignments were finished, of a better life and how I planned to achieve it. This seemed to work well and I continued using the daydreams all through my days at the university. Upon graduating from the university and when I started reaching my goals in life, the daydreams disappeared! I guess I was just too busy.

After I married Joann and our children Elizabeth and Edward were born I began to dream at night. Pleasant dreams about how good our life is. This was a new experience for me. And then like a ton of bricks the "incident" happened.

Now there is no rhyme or reason which dream happens during the night. When the dreams are about Beth, my caregiver or my children, they are pleasant. When they are about my ex-wife Joann or about Butch, the lowlife, the key player who committed that unforgivable act to me, they are nightmares! With my business, which is the biggest part of my life, I am in total control. With these recurring dreams and nightmares that I am plagued with, I have absolutely no decisions in this. I do not know how to deal with this.

The first dream about Joann after we went our separate ways was the beginning. I remember it so vividly! For some weird reason, it was a calming dream about all of the good times we had. I wish it had not ended. Suddenly I woke up! I could not go back to sleep. I tossed and turned to ponder all of the "What if" questions. What if I would have been satisfied with a small local business instead of a nationwide empire? We would have had the same standard of living, but I would have been home almost every night. She would not have had to fill in her alone time in the evenings after our children were grown. What if I would have called her more just to say, "Hello! How is your day? I love you!"? Would any of these things made a difference and changed the outcome??? Depending on what time of night these dreams or nightmares occurred, would determine whether I could go back to sleep or stay awake until it was time for me to get up and start my day. I tried to rationalize why all of this was taking place. It did not matter if I was staying in a nice hotel or sleeping in my bed. Whether I entertained customers the evening before or had a quiet dinner by myself, the dreams and nightmares continued to haunt me!

If there was time and I did fall back to sleep, more often than not I would dream about Butch. Quickly those dreams turned into nightmares. With all of my sources, I had more information on him than I needed or wanted. I had enough money to legally make his life a "living hell." At the time when I rationally retaliated against him, I thought that I dealt with him in the way he deserved. Why am I now becoming dissatisfied with his penalty? Why am I letting him enter into my quiet time? Why am I letting him begin to control my actions or reactions toward him? Then it would be two or three nights without any dreams or nightmares.

I thought I was free from the dreams and out of nowhere and who knows what caused it, I would dream about Beth. Nothing lustful! She is an excellent caregiver along with being a true friend. She makes my life much simpler and easier by running the errands for me that pertain to my personal life and my business.

My sleep patterns are much better in recent nights and what happens again? Joann is back in my dreams. Now the dreams have become nightmares because I am reliving the unforgivable act. It is so real that I wake up in a nervous, cold-sweat condition! I become very angry! How can I get even with her? I toss and turn in bed for what seems like an eternity. I realize that I am still emotionally involved with her and do not want to harm her emotionally, mentally or physically. Now Butch is an entirely different story. What if I do take my anger out on him? He is a parasite to society. No one will care what happens to him and some people will probably be glad when they hear about it. Then I start struggling with my inner being. Why am I letting him control me? Why am I letting him take away my nighttime rest and making my daylight hours harder to get through? Why? Why?? Why?!

Scattered throughout this season of miserable nightmares are the oh so pleasant dreams about my children. How refreshing it is to wake up in the morning after dreaming about Elizabeth and Edward. Somehow I believe these dreams help me to keep going! Why both of them are not in the same dream I will probably never know. The subject matter of the dreams ranges from silly things to serious events to major achievements. Not like the ones with Joann and Butch where it is verbatim scenes over and over and over! I remember waking up laughing when I had dreamed about the time that Edward caught a toad. He put it in Joann's flowerpot on the kitchen sink windowsill. The toad was quite happy living there until Joann watered the plant. I was sitting at the kitchen table drinking coffee when out of nowhere came a blood-curdling scream. I didn't know who wanted out of the kitchen the fastest. Joann or the toad?

Even after the serious dreams about the children, I wake up relaxed. I believe it is because I went back to a place in time where Joann, Elizabeth, Edward, and I were together living a life of happiness. One rare morning when I had a chance to sleep in, the dream was about shortly after Christmas when Elizabeth had earned her driver's license. She ran over Edward's new bicycle while backing out of the driveway. First, there was the sound of the crash followed by screams from both of them at each other! "You need to watch where you are going!" "You need to keep your bicycle off of the drive!" By the time I was outside to referee it was settled. Elizabeth had volunteered to take Edward to the store and with her money replace his bicycle.

If I could, what would I give to replace all of the nagging nightmares about Joann and or Butch with this one about Elizabeth when she walked down the runway with so much grace and beauty to be crowned queen of the debutante ball?

Out of the darkness of night and for no apparent reasons the see-saw nightmares about Joann and Butch returned. I start wondering if I should ask my doctor for a stronger dose of pain medicine?

Chapter 2
CHARLES—HUMBLE BEGINNINGS

"Reading books in the third grade open my eyes and mind to a much bigger world than the small domain that I live in. Also I begin to see how nice some of my classmates are dressed" I ask myself, "How do I get out of this poverty environment into which I was born?"

Growing up in a four-family cold-water flat was not easy for my family and me. We lived on the second floor because the rent was less per month. There was a living room, kitchen, a single bathroom, and two bedrooms. My parents had one bedroom. I and my siblings coexisted in the other. We lived above a grocery store that was located in a converted apartment. The words "cold water" explained it all. Absolutely all the water had to be heated for washing dishes, baths, shaving, house cleaning, and washing clothes.

The old washer, located in the basement, had the exposed wringers which the clothes were fed through by hand. The wringers, two rubber covered rolls, squeezed out most of the rinse water so that the clothes would dry faster. I learned fast where the quick release was at for the wringers in case my hand got caught accidentally while helping my mother. To some the word "mother" is stern. I liked to call her Mother out of love and respect. She worked hard for her children and did the best that knew how. The water for the washer had to be heated in a copper kettle on a homemade gas stove. It took two of us to move the kettle with water in it. With all of the clothes to wash it was a way of life, not a dreaded task. After washing, the clothes were hung on lines inside or outside to dry.

I loved my sisters and brothers. Sharing a single bedroom with them was another story. This left no quiet time which everyone needs once in a while. My fondest memory is when Papa finally saved enough money to buy my mother a modern electric refrigerator. The shipping box was given to me and I moved it to the basement and put it by the coal bin. Yes, a coal bin. The bin or small room stored coal to burn in the furnace to heat our apartment. I made a clubhouse out of the box and scrounged items to decorate it. This quickly became my place to escape and dream of building a better life. The human brain is an amazing thing and all of the memories stored there, good or bad, are incredible. A thought just occurred to me about how we would make snow ice cream. It was simple, fun, and easy to make. What a treat for us. Fresh snow, cream, sugar, and a little vanilla. All you did was place a scoop of fresh snow in a dish and mix the rest of the ingredients in. The trick was to collect the snow early in the morning before it was covered by the ashes from all of the coal furnaces in the neighborhood.

My papa was a cabby and my mother took in washing and ironing to help make ends meet. I was the youngest of five, two brothers and two sisters. There was enough difference in age that I was almost like the start of a second family. I remember people would tease me about being a mistake when I was young. I was unsure of what they meant—some kind of a joke I guessed! My oldest brother died when I was really small. I was too young to know what it was about, except in my mind I can still see my mother holding him and crying and crying. And then he wasn't with us anymore. As I grew older and people would talk about him, the answer was always the same. "He's in a better place." In my simple childhood thinking, I kept wondering why he got to go to a better place and we didn't. After all, we are living in a crowded dingy apartment on the second floor above a busy street. When we would go outside, passersby would make fun of our worn, outdated clothes. Those lessons in life gave me the Incentive to become what I have become.

Papa's schedule as a cab driver stayed the same. He started at 6 am and got off at 5 or 6 in the evening. Mother would try her best to have supper on the table when he got home. On the days that he worked, Wednesday through Sunday, she would cook some meals that could be kept warm on the stove. On occasion, without notice, Papa would be late. When this happened, Mama would always console him by being nice and saying the same thing. "Darling, do not let your anger overtake you because a fair stiffed you!" At that time, the only thing I knew was Papa was late for supper and I was hungry. As I got older, I realized it meant a passenger left the cab without paying and he had to work longer hours to make up for it. This taught me never to steal from someone because of not knowing the domino effect it may have. Another lesson I learned from this was the strong devotion they had for each other and their marriage. It was like that television program, "The Sun Lighters" or something like that. We could not afford a television. On nice evenings, we would gather with other people outside the neighborhood appliance store and watch through the window. I think the main character was a bus driver. I remember on the show he and his wife had their ups and downs, but they always made up. That's how it was with Mother and Papa. Papa would work every Saturday and Sunday for the extra money because the tourists were in town. I couldn't figure out how tourists had more money than we did but I vowed to find out.

On Papa's days off he and my grandpa did handyman jobs for money to help make things better for us. I started working for them when I was eight or nine years old mixing concrete or plaster, sweeping up the sawdust, or throwing away the trash. My grandpa lost a house due to foreclosure during the Great Depression. Their motto was "Owe no man anything!" For them, it meant doing without and waiting patiently until the money was there. This filtered down to me. When I started working for them I made 25 cents per hour. I could walk to the local five and dime and buy the treasures a little boy desires. When I was not working for my papa and grandpa I would sell greeting cards, flower and garden seeds, or all-purpose salve in a can, door to door. I did not receive cash for my efforts. I got to pick an item from the company's list. I remember when I chose a portable radio, mounted it on my bicycle, and rode down the street listening to my favorite songs. No other kid had that luxury unless they were with me. I was learning that my lifestyle could change if I worked for it. By the time I became a teenager my papa and grandpa quit doing the extra jobs. Grandpa was getting old and Papa was worn out.

I had to find another source of income and there was an opening for a paperboy. The route was not very far from our flat. It was delivering papers door to door. What a life lesson! Many of the properties were rentals. One of my unwritten rules was that if no one answered the door, leave a paper and collect the next time. I had to buy my papers ahead of time and collect the money when I delivered them. This came to haunt me in a couple of ways and both cost me money. Some of the renters would move out owing me money. The other was when my mother, papa, and I would take a simple vacation to the country to stay at an old resort. Nothing fancy but it was a vacation! All of this was possible after my sisters and brother moved out and Papa's wages increased. The union he belonged to sure helped him out. I had to have a person fill in for me. The customers wanted their papers. I would explain to my replacement which customers owed me money. When I returned home the answers were the same. My fill-in would tell me that everyone owing you money is waiting to pay you. When I asked the customers for the money, they would reply, "We paid the other boy!" I never did find out who was lying to me! This I did know, I had to sell two papers to make up for each paper I was not paid for. I vowed to myself if I ever have children they will not have a paper route.

I could not afford to go to the movies very often. Every now and then a movie would be showing that I just had to see. "Gone with the Wind" was one of those must-see silver screen productions! No popcorn, pop, or candy. Those items cost way too much! The plantation way of life mesmerized me. Slavery was appalling to me and I thought my life was bad. How can a human being be treated like that? In awe of the mansion, property, and clothes I watched with special attention to Scarlett vowing never to be hungry again. I made up my mind to be a modern-day Rhett Butler when I left home. The reality was my parents and grandparents were modern-day slaves. They barely eked out a living. The only difference was they were not bought and sold on the courthouse steps or physically abused.

Mother would try her best to take us to church on Sunday. Sometimes we had to miss because she had to finish some washing and ironing before Monday. We would go to a little storefront church. Mother would tell us we could only go there. "Why?" some of us would ask.

With a tear in her eye, she would tell us in her best broken English, "We are poor people with used clothes. They don't accept us in their fancy church buildings!" At the mission, they would read out of the good book and sing about better days! I thought all books were good and I certainly anticipated the better days. If things got worse, the next move would be to join my oldest brother in a better place. As I got older, I found out you had to die to get there. Joseph got to go there because Papa did not have money for a doctor.

As a child, growing older, days seemed to pass as slow as watching a fresh coat of paint dry on a bicycle. As time went by, I was allowed to play on the sidewalks and at the local school ground. It was then that I could walk the three blocks to my Grandma and Grandpa Whitford's house. The owners of the grocery store would let me use their telephone long enough to call my grandma to make sure it was ok to visit her. I have many fond memories of my grandparents and what they taught me. Sometimes with words. Sometimes with deeds.

Grandma taught me that most women like flowers. She had two little glass vases that were on the windowsill over her kitchen sink. When I played in her small backyard, I would pick some kind of wildflower and take it to her. It may have been a dandelion, a wild violet, or a white clover bloom. It did not matter to her. She would put it in her little vase with some water, set it on her windowsill, and it would stay there until it wilted.

Grandma also taught me what respect is. This is how she did it. If she was busy doing a chore and I asked for something, she would set a time when she would do what I asked. I learned two things. Not to go ask again and she would keep to her committed time. She had her work to do while Grandpa was at work. She would also set aside some time for fun whenever it was possible. We would move the kitchen chairs into the living room. She would cover the chairs with a couple of bed sheets. That became our clubhouse. She would join me and we would play some kind of make-believe game.

My grandpa worked long hours at his job. He did spend quality time with me. He had a very small shop in their basement. One day, because I asked, he helped me make a fishing pole out of wood. He bent a nail and made a hook. He found some twine for the line. After lunch, we walked to a nearby park so I could try my newly made fishing pole in a stormwater ditch. He knew there were not any fish in the water but he didn't spoil my fun. My love for them never went away and neither will the memories.

Part of growing up is watching what the other children are doing, both the ones who are younger than I am and the others who are older. Strangely, I cannot do what I used to do because I am older. And the opposite side of the coin is that the neighbors older than me are doing things that I cannot do. This perplexing phenomenon seemed to cause time to pass really slow.

The two things that stand out in my memory years later are bicycles and the game of bottle caps. Usually, the bicycles in our neighborhood were owned in a progressive order. I did not get a different bicycle every year. The bike had to last me two or three years. Over time two were purchased from neighborhood boys that had outgrown them. Two were bought from a nearby secondhand store. When I was sixteen I had earned and saved enough money to buy my first new bicycle. I had finally arrived at a different status in my neighborhood.

Back to the game of bottle caps. For several years I had watched the boys and some of the girls play the game. They played on one end of the playground while we played softball on the opposite end. Playing bottle caps worked well for the size of the field. The field was not big enough to play baseball and softball at the same time. It still amazes me how that growing up in that area almost everyone learned to share. I guess it was because all of us were in the same "boat."

The time finally had arrived and I was old enough to play bottle caps with the big kids. I instantly found out how much smaller bottle caps and a broomstick are compared to a softball and bat. We played the game similar to baseball except there were no outfielders. No one could hit a cap past the bases. Some of those pitchers could sail a cap better than a Frisbee. Bottle caps and old broomsticks were plentiful so we never lacked what we needed to play the game. Besides the endless supply of those two items, no gloves were needed. Thankfully no one ever had an eye injury. Thinking about the size of a bottle cap and the speed it was thrown, at my age now, I don't know if I could see one much less hit it.

I learned a lot about life on the playground. Those days taught me that I wanted to stay on the right side of the law. No one sat me down and explained this. The lesson was real. The police would come down the street or to the playground and start talking to people, mostly the older ones. The next thing you knew one or two in the crowd would be handcuffed and put in the squad car. In a day or two, some of them would be back while others never returned. I don't know what happened to them. With little children, it was different. The officer would walk the child home and talk to the parents. And more times than not for the next week or two the only time you saw her or him was at school. Punishment was served by being grounded. Either way, I did not want any part of it.

The most important business principles in life I learned as a kid on the streets. All through the city were highly organized unofficial territories. There was a leader in each territory. He answered to someone, somewhere. Also, the leader had people in the territory doing the work for him. Although I never got involved in this, I fully understood how the system worked. The knowledge of how this system worked established some of my main principles in business. I never sold a product unless I had an ironclad contract for a specific territory and I received commissions on all sales including the sales produced by my staff. And if the supplier wanted me out, they had to buy my contract. Either way, I made money.

Papa died right after I graduated from high school. I helped my mother with the rent by working for the grocery store owner. I made my spending money by tossing nickels in the alley and betting on difficult hoop shots at the local playground. Mother lived long enough to see me graduate from high school and attend one year at the university.

That first year at the university was tough. It was out in the state from New York City. While most students went to school full time and received allowances from home, I took the minimum hours allowed and worked full time sending part of the money to my mother. After she passed away, there was no reason to go back to New York City.

After that, I cut my work hours and concentrated more on my studies. I found additional ways to make money. From my economic background, I learned from Papa, people like us could not borrow money. If we did, the interest would eat you alive. Papa never used a bank. We were so poor, who would think to steal from us? On campus, I did use the bank. It would have been disastrous for me to lose my money. What I did have was money to loan other students on a short term basis for profit. Collecting was easy. There was always a football player or two who would collect a bad loan for fun and a few bucks! Once the word got out, there were not any bad debts.

Another source of revenue that became the most fun was buying and selling items on campus. It seemed like this was a way of life. A student would get a new watch or something for Christmas, a birthday, etc. and would sell the old. I would buy some of the items and resell most of them to turn a profit. I was always careful not to buy stolen goods. I paid informants on campus to listen for stolen or lost goods and report back to me. Lost goods were returned for a reward. More income! The university did not teach me how to make money. The streets of New York City did. What the university taught me was the protocol of dealing with customers and suppliers.

Chapter 3
BUTCH—"WHO CARES?"

Being born into a family that did not want me, I ask myself over and over, "Who really cares about me?"

Growing up for me was very unconventional. I have a brother and a sister. I was born when my brother was thirteen and my sister was twelve. We lived in a modest, clean, and well-maintained house in a neighborhood where most of the men were blue-collar workers at the local mills. A few of the women worked outside of their homes.

It was an old established neighborhood. Like my brother and sister, more often than not, the neighbor's children were much older than I was. There were not many children my age to play with. I had to entertain myself at home. When I would go to the garage or basement where my dad and brother were working on the car or some other project, I was told, "Run along, you are too little to help us!" It was the very same story when I tried to be around my mom and sister.

To add insult to my weary heart, I went to the first meeting at school with my parents. I do not remember what it was for. All of the other students and their parents were there. I found out how cruel my classmates could be. It started at intermission while we were allowed to get out of our seats to have refreshments or to visit. I overheard some of my classmates snickering and making comments about how I lived with my grandparents. Returning to our seats for the remainder of the meeting I started looking around at the adults. Even the students in the higher grades were sitting with adults who appeared to be much younger than my mom and dad. Heartbroken I quietly went home and went to bed. Who could I ask about this? My mom or dad would have told me to "toughen up!" Going to my teacher would not have worked. I knew she had her "pets" because certain students were treated like I saw how my brother and my sister were pampered at home. Church? No way! When the word "church" was mentioned at my house the answer from my dad was always the same. "I work five or six days a week just to provide a roof over your head, food on the table, and clothes for your back. On my one or two days off I am either repairing something or taking a well-deserved break from everything! No, we are not going to church. That is a place for do-gooders who have nothing better to do!"

As time passed, my brother and my sister moved out of my parent's home. Naturally, they would return to visit. After they moved out I thought things would change for me but nothing did. Mom and Dad still did not have time for me. But when my brother or sister stopped by to visit, it was like time stood still and they had never moved out. I came to realize that my mom and dad had two boys, but only one son and that was not me! I learned how to harden my emotions so that I could survive.

Becoming a teenager my world grew larger and larger. I could go to different parts of town and hang out with peers who lived similar lives to mine. It was during one of these journeys that a girl asked the question "Who cares about me?" Riding the bus back home I played those words over and over and over in my mind, "Who cares about me?" Then and there while on the bus I decided that no one cared about me! Absolutely no one! Between my token allowance and saving my lunch money, I had a few dollars for bus fares, a malt, or a must-see movie. I ate two meals at home and skipped lunch at school to keep the money. No matter how hard it was I knew that I had to graduate from high school to get a job.

I persevered and received my diploma. The very next day after graduation I found one of my so-called friends who was fairly good at making homemade tattoos. I had him tattoo on the back of my right hand, WHO and on the back of my left-hand, CARES. When my mom and dad saw the tattoos the verbal fight broke out.

Our relationship, that was nothing, had really deteriorated during my senior year of high school. The biggest reason was due to words spoken by relatives who were visiting my mom and dad one evening. I was in my room studying with the door partially open. Someone asked about the age differences between my siblings and me. Instantly my dad answered. "He was conceived because of a mistake! We never wanted any more children!" I knew then and there it was over.

The next day I talked them into letting me clean out and move into the small apartment above the garage. My dad built it for my brother so when my brother's friends came over they had a place to hang out. A single room with a full bath. Nothing fancy. I would continue to eat meals with my parents not saying a word except, "Thank you," as I went out the door.

After my tattoos healed I began applying for jobs at the local mills. It did not take long to find out it was a waste of time. As soon as the employment office personnel saw the tattoos I heard the standard rehearsed answer. "We will call you when we are hiring." It did not take a rocket scientist to know when they were hiring because the word spread fast on the streets and I was part of the streets.

Wandering around town one day I saw a "Help Wanted" sign in a restaurant window. I didn't even look at the name of the place. I went in, filled out an application, and was hired on the spot to be a busboy. I didn't even know what a busboy did, but I started the next day. The pay was not great but I received a portion of the waitresses' tips which really added up. I was used to getting by with very little money and this was far better than that. The next day when I went to work I looked up and saw the name of the all-night diner. The Majestic.

What a life changer that job was for me. It did not take long for me to understand what my job meant to the waitresses. The faster that I cleaned the tables, the faster new customers could be seated which translated into more tips. That was the name of the game. Then the icing on the cake came along.

In between customers, when things were slow, I began to eavesdrop on the waitresses' conversations. I heard one of them say that her husband had not touched her in weeks because of some off the wall comment she made about his mother. Guess what? When the opportunity would avail I would accidentally bump into her or I would casually touch her hand while handing her plates, etc. Before long I was taking the place of her husband.

From time to time some boyfriend would break up with a waitress with the same old worn-out excuse. "You are not good enough for me" or "I deserve someone who is prettier than you." Guess what again? Along comes Butch with "You are much better than I deserve" or "I have never had a girlfriend as pretty as you." All of this worked much easier than I thought was possible. All of the waitresses had different days off work and because we worked together not a word could be said about our away from work activities! Everyone knew what would happen in the workplace if jealousy erupted. I didn't really care about any of them. For me, it was a place in life that I had never been before. I was in control and I liked the attention.

Chapter 4

Beth—A Soul Afraid Of Being Hurt

With loving and supporting parents, I keep asking myself, "Why did I allow my heart to get so hard?"

From the time I was born until the summer between my junior and senior years in high school, I was a "military brat." I was a single child. My father came from a family rich in military history. No generals, but proud of their service! Sometimes this carried over at home. As his daughter, I learned to live with his military ways. For me, some were good, while others were not.

I do not remember how many times we moved before my father retired. Emotionally and physically I clung to my mother. She was the only constant in my life. When we moved during the school year instantly my friends and classmates were gone. In a quantum leap, I was in a classroom surrounded by new faces. The first and second grades were the hardest because school was new to me. Either I was leaving or some of my classmates were. Our parents were good at writing letters but sooner or later the friendships went by the wayside. Who knows why? Maybe the letters got lost in the mail.

As I grew older I learned to cope with losing friends by not allowing myself to become emotionally attached to anyone except my mother and father. This action worked well to protect me except I could see how my other classmates interacted with each other and I was missing out. I made up my mind that I did not care. It was the lesser of the evils and I was tired of being hurt!

During that summer when my father retired my life changed dramatically. My parents purchased a house in a middle-class neighborhood. That was a big adjustment for me. Stability! That was totally new to me. I saw the same families up and down the street while riding my bicycle or walking my puppy. And a puppy! I never had a pet unless it was a goldfish and you know how short their lifespan is.

While on my walk one day going past a house, three houses down the street from our home, I noticed a teenage boy sitting on the front porch. We halfheartedly smiled and waved at each other and I kept on walking. This would repeat on occasions. Oh no, I told myself, you are not becoming friends with him! You have learned your lessons in the past. The plan worked well because I no longer saw him around the neighborhood. Chalk one up for my side for not allowing someone in my life only to see him leave and for me to get hurt.

The summer went by swiftly. The school year began and with it the memories of the past eleven years. I decided to open my mind a little, just a little, and see what this new life would be? But not dropping my self-learned defense mechanism completely and getting hurt again for who knows how many times?

Walking with the puppy down the street, after school, I saw the boy sitting on the front porch again. I gave him one of those just-barely waves. The kind of wave if he did not acknowledge it I could pull my hand back quickly and keep on walking. He did acknowledge it. He waved back at the same time and said, "Hello!" I smiled back and kept on walking. I thought he was cute and had a nice smile. A couple of days later I devised a plan to stroll by his house without the puppy just in case he was outside. The plan worked. He was by the sidewalk pulling scattered weeds out of the grass. With no puppy to distract me, I mustered enough courage to stop and talk.

He introduced himself to me as Henry or Hank whichever I preferred. He was very polite and we exchanged a few pleasantries. I mentioned that I had not seen him at school and he quickly told me that he graduated last year and was going to a local trade school to be a car mechanic. In his spare time, he worked at an auto parts store to help pay his way through school. Before I could tell my story to him, I heard my mother calling me for supper. As I was leaving, he asked, "By the way, what is your name?"

"Bethany, but my friends call me Beth," I replied.

Several days later there was a knock at the front door. I went to the door and it was Hank. Since my mother and father were at home I invited him in. My father sat and listened more than he said anything. I knew this was his old military training. He was gathering information to make an evaluation. After fifteen or twenty minutes Hank excused himself to go to work. Then came the dreaded silence before my father spoke the words "I like him!" Oh, what a relief!

The next Saturday Hank asked me to go roller skating. I had not been on skates for years. I was not going to let that stop me from going on a date with him. My father was impressed because a time was given when he would pick me up and a time was set when he would bring me home. Hank was punctual. We started dating. Absolutely nothing serious. Just going to fun places three or four times a month. It worked well for me. There was none of that silly teenage jealousy because of dating a person who was an ex-boyfriend of so and so. This was my senior year and it went by fast.

After I graduated I started seeing more of Hank. Now I was eighteen years old. My parents relaxed the rules some. Not much, but some!

During the summer I worked at a flower shop. When fall arrived I enrolled at the junior college and continued to work part-time. What an experience working at the flower shop was, to say the least! I met customers who were from all walks of life. Some were happy while others were sad. Some rich, some poor. Birthday flowers! Funeral flowers! Wedding flowers! Anniversary flowers! Flowers for this! Flowers for that! After the first day, I knew I had to put back in place that old defense mechanism to keep my distance from the customers. I could not let my customers give me free tickets to ride their emotional carousel! Over time, delightfully, things were getting really serious with Hank. He asked me to marry him. I accepted and we set our wedding date for June following my graduation with an associate degree.

Our wedding was picture perfect. We chose to have a simple wedding in a park under a gazebo where Hank and I spent some time while we were dating. The temperature was just right and there was not a cloud in the sky. Only the intermediate family and a few close friends attended. I was still working at the flower shop. This provided an inside track to the most beautiful flowers. Their fragrance permeated the area and nature provided her best with the birds singing. The reception was totally different and I thought the whole world was there. Some were people that I did not know. It was held at a local veteran's hall. Nothing fancy, but very clean. A good time was had by all from the youngest to the oldest. The meal, the band, and the drinks. Wow! There was a snow cone machine for the youngsters. Now and then I saw an adult sneak over to the bar with a plain snow cone and had the bartender add a secret flavor to it.

I was never happier in my life. For once, besides my parents,

I had someone that I cared for and Hank certainly cared for me. I applied for an entry-level job at the Garden of Eden and was accepted. The Garden of Eden was an above-average assisted living facility. It was there I chose to become really hard-hearted. Unlike my classmates who moved away, these people passed away!

The owner of the car parts store expanded his business and promoted Hank to manager with a substantial raise in pay. With this, Hank chose to drop out of trade school and not become a mechanic.

Like most married couples Hank and I rented an apartment for the first couple of years we were married. Then the timing was perfect. While we were looking for a house to buy, a house came on the market in the next block from our parents in our old neighborhood. We looked at the house and purchased it. Hank and I were like two teenagers who were having fun while building a clubhouse in the backyard except we were married. We were giddy as we painted the rooms and just happened to flip a little paint at each other. Once we settled in, how special it was to stroll down the street. Sometimes we would stop and visit our parents. While at other times we walked and enjoyed our time together reminiscing about how we met. Several years went by. Hank and I were doing well. We knew it was time to start our family.

As soon as I was pregnant Hank and I began to turn one of the three bedrooms into a nursery. What a joy it was to shop for furniture, curtains, and the necessities. I did not believe how fast the nine months passed. The decorating, the shopping, and the two baby showers. My mother and mother-in-law held the first shower for me. The biggest surprise was who gave the second shower for me. The residents of the Garden of Eden. The very people that I had deliberately set a social distance between them and me. It was humbling but I did not drop my defense mechanism.

May was our firstborn. Ella was born two years later and it

was like time stood still. Hank and I chose those names because of two elderly ladies in the neighborhood. They were always kind to us. Both were widowers and neither had children. They would bring homemade candies, breads, and doughnuts to us. We in turn invited them over for dinner and to play cards. The turning of the third bedroom into a nursery was as exciting as the first time. The shopping, showers, and most of all the anticipation. I continued to work at the Garden of Eden.

Chapter 5

Edward—A Natural Born Environmentalist

Many times and I do not have the answer, I ask myself, "Why was I blessed to have such wonderful parents?"

Since I have not been home for quite a while, I arrived a couple of days early to prepare for the funeral and take a walk through our old neighborhood. Not much has changed. I have not mastered the English Language well enough to do justice to paint pictures with words of the home that I considered a privilege of growing up in. Our parents were not perfect and neither was my sister. Don't ask her, I think to myself because the answer will be biased and distorted as I laugh! Their imperfections were far outweighed by their unconditional love and their encouragement for my sister and me to become what we were created to be. Being the only son born into an affluent family meant that I was expected to follow in my father's footsteps. This means taking over the reins of his business when he retires. Early on, my parents had the insight this would not happen. I would not be pushed into something I did not want. My sister put all of her efforts into becoming a business owner like our father. Going against tradition Elizabeth was encouraged to be a business owner and I was allowed to explore the botanical side of nature.

At the far end of our backyard were trees and beyond the trees was a small creek large enough to wade in. That was fun. There I was exposed to fish, turtles, frogs, insects of all kinds, and a snake now and then. All of these creatures fascinated me, but not as much as plants. From that exposure to nature I knew what I wanted to do in life; work with nature and raise plants. After a few discussions with my father he agreed to let me dig up a small plot in the backyard and I planted gardens every year until I moved out. The only requirement was that I could not plant an aggressive plant that would harm the grass, the flowers, or the trees.

Years ago looking through a magazine one day I read an article about the benefits of composting. On the last page, there was information on where to order plans from an article titled, "How to Build a Compost Bin." I saved my allowance and ordered the plans. To this day I can remember how excited I was when the packet arrived in the mail and my father, without hesitation, agreed to help me build the bin. The following Saturday he took me to the local lumber yard and bought the material. I was amazed at how skilled he was and how fast he completed the project. I commented to him about this.

My father's explanation became engraved in my heart! He told me how he grew up helping his papa and grandpa do odd jobs for extra money to meet their financial needs. He further explained that in his world of business he earned more money closing a deal in the same amount of time it would take to complete projects around the house and property. Knowing this, he paid people to do this work while he expanded his customer base. I asked him, "Then why are you helping me to build the bin?"

He instantly replied, "It is not about the money son, it is

showing that I believe in you!" I will never forget that. What a great life lesson taught so very simply.

I walk down the sidewalk so that I can look in the backyard. The compost bin was gone and had been replaced by a swing set. I did notice one thing that was still there. It is a concrete pad that my father saved scrap metal on. My father participated in the recycling process years before it became a way of life. He taught this to me at an early age. He would pick up scrap metal that he saw placed along the streets. He had me go through the neighborhood the day before trash pickup to see what I could find and bring home. He certainly did not need the money. He did not care what the neighbors thought about it. Recycling was good for the environment and he was proud to be a part of the program. When he and I would accumulate a set amount of scrap, it was a tradition on a Saturday morning just before lunch to take it to the scrapyard and sell it. For some reason, he and I did not go straight home. The next stop would be at the dairy bar for burgers and malts. Oh, how I miss those days!

Instead of playing sports, I liked to be alone watching plants, learning how and why they grow. The closest thing I did to participating in sports was shooting pool with my father. Without saying, the best part was our time together. We always played the game of 8-ball. The biggest lesson that he taught me was the game was not over until one of us won! It did not matter if he was winning and how bad he was beating me, the game was not over until a winner was declared. Just like the "game of life," how true it is! The lessons the game itself taught me were to plan ahead, to be patient, to evaluate the situation, and to change my strategy if necessary, to change the outcome. I applied all of these to my life and especially to raising plants.

Our father hired a yard crew to take care of our property.

Knowing my interest in plants they found small tasks for me to do. As each year passed the tasks became harder and took more skill to accomplish. After the crew finished their weekly work I would go stand across the street and admire our work. I learned what I needed to know about planting grass seed, repairing bare spots, mowing the correct way to show off the grass, and trimming trees, shrubs, and roses. I realized this was what I wanted to do in life. No college for me and my parents blessed my decision. After graduating from high school I was hired full time by the yard crew my parents used. The work was extremely rewarding! During the warm months, we worked six days a week, eight to ten hours a day. That is when I saved money to take me through the winter.

Later I moved to the Gulf Coast for full-time year-round work. The different species of plants perked my interest in nature even further. The "no college for me" quickly went out the window. I earned my degree going to school at night. Now I do freelance work developing a variety of plants for an international seed company. My parents led by example. What more can I ask for?

Chapter 6

ELIZABETH—LIKE FATHER, LIKE DAUGHTER

"I did not know what was going on in my father's life!" I ask myself, "How did I become that busy?"

I was distraught after my father called me and asked that I come for the sale of our family home in two weeks. My father and I always had an open line of communication between us. To my surprise and disappointment this time he would not tell me why he was selling our home. I pleaded with no avail. I could not be at the sale. I had a booth at a home show to take reservations for my resort and to sell condos in my high rise on the beach.

I was blessed with parents that created me and raised me to be a responsible adult. As a child, I came to know this by being around other children at school, on the playground, or from life in general. Some of my friends or girls who I knew had to wear hand me down clothes from older siblings. Not me! I was the firstborn and only girl.

Yes, we did have a girls-only clubhouse. At a few of those girls-only meetings, I tried to forget what was said. While most of the conversations were silly fun girl stuff a couple of girls cried when they told what happened to them at home or a relative's house. How terrible! We consoled them the best we could and asked them to talk to the school principal or nurse. Whether they did or not, we never knew. We would not bring up the subject for fear of embarrassing them. I was always so thankful that nothing like that happened to me. My home was a safe haven and I was always treated with respect. I grew up admiring my father. He was kind of "standoffish." I knew this. I also knew how much he loved me and that he never neglected his family's needs.

He had his own business and did well with it. He was constantly traveling leaving on Monday or Tuesday and returning home on Thursday or Friday. He was always home on weekends and holidays. This was cast in stone family time.

Holidays were my father's favorite times of the year. His enjoyment of the holidays superseded his work. We celebrated each one in a special way and that could change from year to year. Not Thanksgiving or Christmas. The rituals for these two were cast in stone. They were very traditional and I gratefully participated in the activities. The Christmas season held a place in my father's heart that would never change. I think it was his favorite time of the year while he was growing up. As soon as Thanksgiving was over he invited a Baptist minister to our house for dinner. He pastored the church where the Christmas carolers attended that would stop by our house and sing. I knew Father looked forward to listening to their carols.

The main topic of conversation during the evening when the minister was there was to discuss which two families we were going to share some Christmas joy with. We were given the names, genders, and ages of the family members. As we shopped for our Christmas presents we would shop for their presents and food for them. A week before Christmas we would deliver all the items to the church without any of our names. Sometimes my father would have a live tree, lights, and ornaments delivered to someone's home. Father always wanted people to have a better Christmas. I learned this lesson well.

Because of my father's business, I looked forward to Mondays. Being the first day of the school week, the teacher would ask me to tell the class all the places he had been the past week. The discussions were not about his business. The intention of our teacher was to enlarge our small developing world by letting our little minds wander. She was so gifted at guiding us out of our cocoons and helping us to become what we were created to be. It was great to have a teacher who used her talents in such an admirable profession.

Growing up with a younger brother was fun. I am five years older than he is. By being a different gender and the age gap between us there was very little competition. My interests and his were 180 degrees apart! I wanted to be an extrovert like my father and deal with people. Edward, on the other hand, thoroughly enjoyed watching and learning about nature with no humans involved! I think our biggest and most often fusses, not fights, were over who got to lick the beaters or scrape the cookie dough out of the mixing bowl. Mother had a real knack for keeping this under control. In some mysterious way, she could remember who did what last time!

I watched my father and gleaned everything that I could from him. I wanted my own business when I became an adult, not his business. I took the correct classes all the way through school and I was very active in the performing arts. I performed every chance that I could whether it was in a high school production or at the town's theatre. I was a varsity cheerleader in my junior and senior years for the basketball and football teams. I was groomed to be a debutante at the annual ball my senior year and I was ready to play the part. Upon graduating from my parents' alma mater I was ready to enter the business world. I wanted to sell insurance and real estate. Father encouraged me to get my broker's licenses for both while I was going to the university. It was hard, but the rewards surely followed. I was ready to hit the road at full speed the week after I was out of school. How wise was his advice!

It was a given that I did not want to live in the city. My father and I would take weekend trips up to three hours away to survey the opportunities. I watched my father in action as we ate at the off the beaten path diners, bought a few items from the mom-and-pop grocery stores, browsed the general stores, and hung out at the bowling alleys on Saturday nights. His insight gave to me a quantum leap into the business world in the locale that I chose.

I learned many life lessons from my father. Most of them pertained to interactions with other people. At the top of his list and he definitely practiced this one was that every person you meet in life is for "A Reason, for A Season, or for A Lifetime!"

Father was very faithful at giving real-life examples to me. This philosophy he brought to life with a story that involved him on one Christmas Eve afternoon. During the morning, Mother had asked him to go to a department store and buy some odds and ends. She wanted these items so she could put the finishing touches on the decorations in our home before the guests arrived for our Christmas dinner. He procrastinated until after lunch and time began to run out. When he finally decided to leave it started raining. The entire family knew that he was unhappy, but the person he was, he only blamed himself.

Father arrived home 45 minutes later than it should have taken and with an incredible story. He was walking through the parking lot and saw a man trying to change a flat tire. No big deal right? Wrong! This man was a double amputee at the hips and did not have the strength to loosen the lug nuts. My father stopped in the cold December pouring rain on a Christmas Eve afternoon and changed the tire for him. My father's clothes were soaking wet. He did not care. He calmly told us if he had gone to the store when my mother asked him, he would have missed this opportunity to help this man. This meeting was for "A Reason" He was also very fast to add that the interactions between himself and me, between Edward and him, between our mother and him were for "A Lifetime!" I can never repay him for this.

Chapter 7
Joann—A Spoiled Rich Kid

"Being rich, I do not ask myself anything about my actions. I basically do what I want to!"

I grew up carefree and in a world of privilege. Not because of race, but because of wealthy parents. I watched numerous people grow older. Some were happy while others were sad! Some were vibrant and full of life. Some sat on the doorstep waiting for the Grim Reaper to show up. I never understood what caused the difference? As a child, I would ask my mother what the future held for me? Her answer always came back in a song. I do not remember the title of the song or the name of the recording artist, only a few words from it. "The future's not ours to see, Que sera sera...." Looking back at my younger years, I see what a spoiled brat I was because of who my parents were and how much money they had.

To pass the time when I was not in school or participating in school activities, my mother and father would allow me to work in one of our convenient stores. Basically, I did token tasks. After all, we had hired help to do the work. I absolutely refused to work at the stores in the poverty-stricken neighborhoods. Can you imagine being in the same store with those people? I chose to work in the stores where the well to do did their shopping. Who knows when I would need someone to pull some strings so that I could get what I wanted! It was amazing how we catered to those rich folks. At the stores located in the affluent areas, clerks would pump the gas for them. At the other stores, customers had to pump their own gas no matter how disagreeable the weather was.

The money was collected from all of the stores and brought to a central location for verifying the totals and preparing the bank deposits. The locations would change randomly for security purposes. As I was counting money from the poverty stores one evening I had a real eye-opening thought! The money taken in from these stores equaled the revenue from the other stores in the middle and upper-class areas. The bank credited our accounts and never asked which store the money came from. How did I develop this mindset? I have been reaping the rewards from those people that I looked down upon! How terrible!

Several years later in my mind, I can still vividly picture the house, the yard, and the street where I grew up. It was always a pleasant drive home no matter where we had been. The house was located in the "old money" part of town which by design was in an isolated area. It was a private community. The street was wider than most with a green space and trees in the center to divide the one-way streets. Of course, there was no on-street parking!

The house was two stories built on a large plot of land with old and stately oak trees. No one really knew how old the trees were, only that they had been there forever. On the first floor of the house were the living room, the kitchen with a breakfast nook, the library, my father's office, and the formal dining room. The dining room was my favorite room. The table was made out of walnut and so were the fourteen chairs. It was large enough that six people could be seated down each side and Mother and Father would take their places at the ends. And to show off Mother's antique china, silverware, and crystal glasses was a built-in cabinet, with glass insert doors, custom made to match the table and chairs.

Leading to the upstairs was an open staircase with balusters and handrails handcrafted out of cherry wood. As a little girl, I dreamed of having my wedding pictures taken on the steps and my father made sure it came true! Upstairs were four bedrooms and each had a full bathroom. Can you imagine scheduling bathroom time with your parents and your sister?

My parents have not aged well and their failing health has caused them to leave their cherished home and move into assisted living quarters. It is working for them, but not near the grandeur of the lifestyle they were accustomed to! But what an amazing place to grow up in! I was thinking about an incident at my parent's home that happened during a sunny fall afternoon.

There was a young man who worked for my mother to help pay his way to the local college. He did the day to day outside simple tasks taking care of the house and the property. Ranking firewood, raking leaves, washing windows, trimming Ivy, etc. One day he was in the backyard raking leaves. My nephew was playing catch with a ball by himself. My sister was watching him out of the kitchen window. Her son tossed the ball too far and it rolled over to where the hired help was working. The young man tossed it back to my nephew and they started playing catch. She saw her son playing catch with the young man. My sister exclaimed, "Do you see my son playing with the hired help? After all, we were descendants of a well to do family and I am married to a high ranking military officer." She made up her mind to put a stop to this! She went outside in a huff. Naturally, I followed her. She grabbed my nephew by the arm and she told him, "You do not play with the hired help!"

I will never forget what the young man asked her in a kind,

but very stern way. "Do you think your son playing catch with the hired help is going to contaminate him?" Over the years I have come to realize that I was no better than he was. Without a doubt, I had access to more money and a better lifestyle. I absolutely did not do any yard work. He was a human being just like me!

Chapter 8

Joann's Exile—Obey Or Lose My Inheritance

On my way to Paris, I ask myself, "How did I think that I could have an affair with a commoner and get away with it?"

It is a late afternoon flight. The 747 pushes back from the gate and taxis down the runway to be cleared for takeoff. Once in the air, I am able to relax; somewhat that is! The past month has been very traumatic. What had been a good marriage came to an abrupt end, almost as fast as an abortion can end a pregnancy.

Life for me has always been good and will always be good because of my family's pedigree. I was born into a family with old money on both sides. My mother comes from a long line of politicians living in the county seat which creates an atmosphere that reeks of power, money, and energy. My father's grandfather purchased the first automobile dealership in our town. He and his heirs were on the leading edge expanding that business into taxi cabs, tow trucks and service stations. What foresight! The old full-service gas stations are long gone, but being in prime locations my father's generation turned them into modern-day quick stores. Cash cows we call them!

With the setting sun and the hum of the engines, I fall asleep. The voices of the flight attendants cause me to wake up. I order a double scotch with water. I need something to soften my anxiety. Butch used to help me with his little white pills.

Butch is gone and so are the pills. The pills weren't strong. He stole them from his elderly parents. I think the doctor prescribed them just to appease Butch's mother. I finish my drink and order another one. After all, the flight to Paris is a long one.

I am not happy about my family exiling me. At the same time, I understand. This has been going on for years in high-society families. Heaven forbid that a family name would be tarnished by an unwed pregnancy or some type of disability. That's why the well-heeled people have relatives everywhere. Not really! It sounds good when someone has to disappear for a while.

I took a leave of absence from the university to move to Paris to become an artist. I cannot draw a decent stick person which makes it hilarious. What a great story to hide my intentional acts of indiscretion with Butch, which is the reason for the quick and undisputed divorce from Charles.

I fall asleep. I start dreaming. It is a pleasant dream from my childhood. The 1st-grade teacher asked the students to stand, introduce themselves, and explain how they were given their names. I did not know. I had always been Joann. After school, I asked my mother. She chuckled and proceeded to tell me it was a compromise with my grandmothers. Jo came from Josephine and Ann came from Ann Marie.

The jolt from flying into an air pocket brings the dream to an end. The attendants are serving dinner. I politely refuse thinking I will go back to sleep. With the cabin lights on and passengers talking while eating their meals, that does not happen. The seat next to me is empty so that makes it more comfortable. I turn and stare out the window. It is a clear night and the only lights

I can see are from the plane, the stars and an occasional ship. I start thinking about how I met Charles. He and I met at the university. Both of us were seniors. My degree was in education, his was in marketing which was natural for him. I had seen him in the library several times. He was always by himself studying. I finally decided to interrupt his studies and introduce myself. In the course of the conversation, I learned he was from New York City, had only an average high school education, and had to work to pay his way through school. I respected him for this. No wonder he had to study. My expenses were paid for by Grandmother Ann Marie's trust. Classes were easy for me coming from a private day school. Charles and I started dating. I was surprised that on occasions that some students would come up to us and pay Charles a sum of money. At first, I didn't say anything. But as I got more emotionally attached, I had to find out about this money. Was it from fencing stolen goods? Was it from doing papers for other students? Wrong! None of the above but Charles would never tell me!

After graduation, Charles accepted a job from a local industrial supplier as a salesman. No surprise there. The surprise was that we kept dating. He was not even close to what my parents were expecting for a future son-in-law. They expected a future son-in-law to be born with a golden spoon in his mouth, no exceptions!!! He knew it would take his best sales pitch to be allowed to marry into my family and he pulled it off! I was amazed! That impressed me even more. As our children grew older, I went back to school and obtained my master's degree. I started teaching at my alma mater and earned my doctorate.

The copilot announces over the intercom we are halfway to Paris and the weather is rainy. I fall back asleep. When I awake my mind goes directly to Butch. Why Butch? He was a trivial player in my life but somehow caused the most grief!

My work schedule at the university did not matter. Charles traveled with his business during the week. One night after class, I was invited by a few of my students to an all-night diner named The Majestic. Who names an all-night diner the The Majestic? I agreed to go. No day classes the next day and it would give me a glimpse into the lives of my students. Fascinating to say the least! In between conversations I was taking random glances at the busboy. He may have been 20 or 24. There was something distinctly different about him. Then I figured it out. He had a carefree attitude. Somehow he managed to remain aloof whether the boss was screaming, he broke a dish, or a waitress was on his case. How did he do it? The last time I lived like that was when I was a sophomore at the university. I joined a sorority. All the members including me developed an "I don't care attitude about life." Maybe it was because we had the freshman year in and weren't close enough to graduation to worry about it. Who knows? Who cares? It has been so long ago. I do not know if this carefree attitude is what attracted me to him. It was almost like the night I lost my virginity at a sorority party. Everyone was drinking, not in excess, just enough to amplify the "I don't care" attitude. I didn't even know the guy's name. It didn't matter. I'm a rich girl. I don't need to be a virgin when I get married! That's overrated anyway OR IS IT??

The cabin lights have dimmed. I doze off to the hum of the engines. When I wake up Butch is on my mind again. How am I going to get rid of this person I had chosen to use. My mind drifts back to why I started going to the diner when I knew my students would not be there. I would intentionally sit at a table next to one that needed to be bussed. That is when the small talk with the busboy began and how I learned his name was Butch. By listening to the waitresses, I found out his schedule. I showed up one night just as he was walking across the parking lot. We stopped and talked. The conversation was not going to end so he invited me to his place.

In his apartment, I saw that nothing mattered to Butch. It was clean but plain as a city sidewalk. I stayed for about an hour.

The next week I went to the diner as planned. I was nervous. Butch noticed this and I was totally surprised. He offered me some little pills. Oh no, I refused! I will not be a part of the illegal drug industry. He laughed and told me he stole them from his mom. That made them easier to take. Why? I don't know, but it did. They worked. A couple of hours later I left. The next week the plans changed. I met Butch at his place after he got off work. Again, I was nervous. Butch had more pills. My intentions played out! Within an hour, we were in bed having sex. Nothing fantastic! Just kind of ho-hum, but for some very strange reason, I wanted it to happen again. Who knows why and I certainly did not care! The next week I picked him up after work and drove to my house. I wanted more of him to find out if it would be better in my bed. He agreed and hid in the backseat of my car until we were safe in my attached garage. After all, Charles was out of town and I did not want the neighbors to see Butch.

All of a sudden I am bounced back to reality. The plane's tires have hit the runway. I am in Paris.

My life in Paris would have been the envy of my sorority sisters and a grand time if it had not been forced upon me, had happened before I married Charles, and before I had our children. Being what it is I could have rebelled, taken a stand, and never abided by my family's judgment pronounced upon me. If I had refused the punishment handed down I would have been disinherited. That would have been a financial nightmare and disaster. After all, a good marriage came to a crashing end and my children are not allowed to speak to me. Why be stubborn and lose everything? I have made some errors in judgment, but this is not going to be another one! In a few years, someone else in the family will make a bigger mistake or what appears to be and I will be back in good graces like nothing ever happened!

Since this is the case, why not enjoy my life in Paris? I can choose to be miserable or I can choose to be happy! I will choose to be happy!

When I found out that I was being exiled to Paris by family decree it was bittersweet for me. The family had held court and my sentence is to live in Paris for an undetermined time. So, I decided I would become a Parisian! I packed only one suitcase with just enough clothes and makeup to meet my needs until I went shopping. Not completely trusting the airline personnel, I carried my jewelry given to me from Charles and some safely guarded love letters from him in my purse. He did not write often, but when he did, it kindled a fire in my soul! Letters from when we were dating at the University up until two weeks before my acts of indiscretion. I will guard these letters with my life and never part with them!

My new home is an apartment located above an upscale fashion boutique in a highly desirable area. I can walk to the stores and buy everything that I need. Owning a car is useless. There are numerous sidewalk cafes and restaurants close within walking distance of where I live. Very seldom do I cook. Life is outstanding. I have a balcony overlooking the street and it is large enough for a small table and two chairs. Wow, what a view of Paris and especially the lights at night.

On a nice evening, my favorite thing to do is sit on the balcony, sipping a glass of French wine, and listen to the clamor below. At the time I did not realize studying French in high school and college would come in so handy. On one particular night, for some reason, the airplanes flying in and out catch my attention. I start thinking about Charles and my acts of indiscretion! Oh, how I miss him and my children, Elizabeth and Edward. I wonder how they are doing? All of a sudden a truck "backfires" and jolts me back to reality. I am alone and living in Paris, France. It is time to go in and get ready for bed. I make for myself a double scotch with water. I finish the first and drink a second. I will be out for the night. Tomorrow will be a new day! A chance to start over, to make new friends, and to find some direction for my life. Before I fall asleep, I ask the same question over. "How many new days do I need for this to happen?"

Chapter 9

CHARLES SELLS THE PROPERTY—NOT BY CHOICE

"My parents were poor! I have worked hard for everything that I have! I have been good to people!" I ask myself, "Why is this happening to me?"

The night before the sale of the property I tossed and turned while trying to sleep. I am out of bed way before dawn! "Mr. Whitford," says the auctioneer. I interrupt her. Please call me Charles. She replies, "Charles, you are anxious about nothing! Let me do my job!" She does not have a clue why the house and my belongings are being sold.

My eyes and mind drift back and forth from the driveway below to the horizon while half-heartedly peering out of the upstairs window. It is a crisp sunny November day. At times the sale of the personal property seems to go at warp speed, then without a warning, it comes to screeching halt.

My mind keeps drifting back to the past of all the happy times that had taken place in our home and the effort it took to acquire the earthly goods for my family to enjoy.

I am amazed at the crowd. People from out of state and who

knows where? They start gathering well before the auctioneer is ready to start. What a following this woman has! After all, that is her job to drum up the hype. Working on commission, the higher the sales dollars at the end of the day, the more she earns. Who cares what an item is worth? The job of the "ringer" is to raise the price of each item to what the market will bear.

I curiously watch the auctioneer hawk my belongings. I wonder why Mrs. Jones, my neighbor, bought this and that after she asked Mrs. Smith down the street "Can you believe the dastardly way Mrs. Whitford decorated her home?" While possessions are being sold I ask myself, "Why doesn't someone buy that? Don't they realize what it took to get that out of the Soviet Union, or England, or Africa?"

I am furious as I watch the auctioneer's assistants throw these unsold items into the dumpster. That was the deal. Before I leave the premises today, all personal property is to be sold or destroyed before the house is sold today. My blood is boiling! Knowing before the sun will set, my bank account will be larger, but no '57 Vette, no motorcycle, no pickup truck, and no home. All I will leave with is my clothes, my jewelry, my business computer and papers, items wrapped in old newspapers secured with twine, and my car.

I will not miss the truck. It was useful at the time for doing things around the house and property. Sometimes it was a nuisance having the only truck in the neighborhood. Someone would want to borrow it or would ask me to haul things. The most fun was using it to bring home the fresh-cut Christmas trees or take firewood to Elizabeth and Edward who were ice skating on the local lake. The fire kept the skaters warm with a bonus of roasting hot dogs and marshmallows. I was a hero for bringing the wood and Joann was the heroine for making plenty of hot chocolate!

As I finally drive away, I look in the rearview mirror at my former home and the beautiful sunset. The colors of the sky ease my mind of the emotional turmoil. During what should have been a 30-minute drive to my new residence, but took three times as long, I fondly reflect on my ex-wife, our children, my acquisitions, and my highly successful business. Then like a stealth bomber attack, the negative thoughts materialize of why today had taken place and where I am going. As good as I physically feel, how can I be terminally ill? The doctors could be wrong. How many times have you heard about mistakes being made or a divine miracle that completely defied all the odds of the medical field?

When emotions are involved in a person's life who knows what the thoughts will be? Such is the case while driving to my new residence. Purposefully I take the very long route. I think about a few items that were sold today. For Edward, it was the thoughts of joy revolving around the pool table. Playing the game of 8-ball was our alone time. This was a chance for me to be a responsible father and teach him life lessons. I knew he learned at least one. Do not quit until the game is over. I watched him apply that to raising plants. Until a plant was completely dead he would tend to it hoping it would gain a new life. The sale of my office furniture was bittersweet. It was in my office where Elizabeth and I bonded. She wanted to follow in my business footsteps and I made sure it happened. My new residence has built-in office furniture so it is a total waste of space to take any of it with me. With anger, I had watched the men load up the bedroom furniture that had belonged to Joann and me. Not so much that it was sold, but the event that prompted me to sell the beautiful handmade pieces. Then I thought about the truck.

Who knows why—the truck? The truck caught the eyes of numerous people while I was driving it. It was almost like a luxury car on a truck frame. Shiny jet black with polished chrome wheels. A Sunday morning ritual of mine before Joann and the children got out of bed, was to drive the truck to the convenience store for the weekend paper and a cup of coffee. Now and then I would buy doughnuts for the family depending on what Joann wanted to have for breakfast. I guessed the age of the female clerk who worked the Sunday day shift to be in her mid-twenties. Every Sunday looking at her makeup and clothes, she appeared to have arrived at work straight from a Saturday night party she had attended. She was always polite, clean, but never friendly. It was forever, "Thank you, sir."

The Sunday that I drove the vibrant red "57" Vette with wire-spoke wheels to the convenience store our relationship on her part completely changed. She was the same Saturday night left-over. Immediately I became "Honey." It was, "Hi, honey, will there be anything else for you?" Without any effort, the thoughts came to my mind. I am the same person. My purchases seldom deviated week to week. I always paid cash. Now I was "Honey" because of a vehicle. Oh, well! Who knows where I could have ended up?

I arrive at the Garden of Eden assisted living facility. I park my car, look around and finally walk in. I am warmly greeted by the staff and promptly check in. After all, why should check-in take long? I was already pre-approved and it is down to the formality of signing the final papers. The doorman offers to help move my belongings to my room. I politely refuse. If the world would only understand I am hedging my bets against the doctor's diagnosis and prognosis! In the professional sales world, hedging bets is a way of doing business and I transferred that over to my personal life.

Piece by piece I carry things in and organize my suite exactly the way I want it. The furniture is not quite to my liking, but "so what!" The only time that I will be staying here is to drift in, reorganize, and then back on the road to service customers. As I am looking over the counter space, I pick up the weekly schedule of events. Every day, breakfast, lunch and dinner at the same time. How boring! The local glee club will perform Tuesday evening. That will be Ft. Worth for me this week. Who wants to play bingo Wednesday? A third of the players can't see well and another third can't hear very well! I guess I should be thankful they are doing something they like to do! What the rest of the week holds, right now I do not know. I throw the schedule in the trash and think about running my business. What a waste of a good tree—that paper!

My Sundays are the same. Reviewing and organizing presentations for the meetings, watching enough Sunday sports and news to carry on conversations with the customers, and packing the clothes for the week. Packing was the hardest part of Sunday. This week I was flying Dallas-Ft. Worth, then to Phoenix, on to Los Angeles, and back home Friday afternoon.

Several weeks go by and after what seems like an eternity the court date for the divorce comes to pass. During the divorce proceedings, I am numb! After the legal papers are signed and the dust settles I put more and more time into my business to fill the voids that are in my life. I certainly do not need the money. The hard work of the past is paying off in leaps and bounds with long term contracts, an endless trail of purchase orders, and everyday trips by the accountant to the bank to make deposits. But my alone time is becoming unbearable!

As I am beginning to accept this lifestyle forced upon me. I discover Monday through Friday is fine. It is Friday evening until Monday morning that takes its toll. I think I heard a song about that. I find the easiest and quickest way to fill some of the voids are the bright lights and the noise from the jukeboxes in the bars.

This is getting old very fast. Not that the people are wrong with their agenda, but their agenda is not mine!

While visiting a neighboring town I learn of a singles group that holds their meetings on Saturday afternoons at a church so I give it a try. I drift in and out depending on business trips and the mood I am in. I discover the members are divided up into three groups. The first group has been there forever. They are self-employed and this place provides a constant supply of newly divorced people. It is proclaimed these people can be trusted having been divorced just like you. I know this group will never find someone and have to leave this direct path of new customers. The second group gives good testimonies about how they want their lives to change. I never see any actions to endorse this desired new life. Maybe they do not know how? The third group is as afraid as I am. I drop out and go back to filling my alone time with work. I learned hard work pays from my papa and grandpa.

Chapter 10
CHARLES' LIFE GOES ON—PLAY THE CARDS YOU ARE DEALT

"Many years ago I learned to play the cards that I am dealt in life." I quit asking the question, "Why have I been dealt this hand?"

The weekly business rituals have been completed as planned. A few bumps in the road, but life is not about the bumps but how you recover. The contract that I had my mind set to finalize in Dallas-Ft. Worth did not happen. Somehow I missed a key point. The good news is the client was impressed enough to postpone her decision for a week in order for me to resubmit my proposal.

Phoenix was more laid back. Servicing this account was a dream. It is a third-generation family-owned business and a terrific partnering program between them and me. November, by their choice, is the month that our meetings are scheduled to reflect on the success and pitfalls of the present year along with finalizing the opportunities and discussing the challenges of the upcoming year.

On to Los Angeles. LA is what it is all about. The hunt! The presentation! The kill! I nail it!!! That sums up a salesperson's life. Now comes the hard part of keeping what the client thought was said. For real estate, it is said to be location, location, location! For me, it is perception, perception perception. Now I am smart enough to know you have to have a good product and good service to back it up. But a larger than life perception is what makes a superstar!

The flight home is uneventful. During a two-hour weather delay, I make the best of it. I relax, make telephone calls, and make plans for next week. To me, I travel to make money. You should hear all of the moaning and groaning from the vacationers and unseasoned travelers. Because of the miles I travel each year, I am for erring on the safe side. Where is the logic to take off on time and then crash? I guess for some if that would happen, they would not get to complain about a flight delay! Oh well, sooner or later we will take off and the negative people go on to trashing something else they don't have a clue about. If only they could be as smart as they think they are! They would be some wizards!

Arriving at the Garden of Eden, nothing's changed. I look at next week's schedule of activities. Ditto, ditto, ditto! I am thinking, "How come the residents cannot memorize this schedule?" For crying out loud, let's save a tree and shortchange the landfill. Then I suddenly stop and realize that many of the residents are not blessed with the mental capabilities that I have!

There is a knock at the door. I am not expecting any visitors. Opening the door, I see it is Bethany. She is a pleasant young lady (around 30) who works at the facility. Her duties are strictly public relations and housekeeping. Politely, but firmly, I stress the points that she is doing an outstanding job of housekeeping; plenty of towels, dishes are washed, and the bathroom is kept immaculate!

Next week is Thanksgiving already. Since the very silent divorce and the recent sale of the property along with moving, I am not emotionally ready to face any of the family. Since I will be in Dallas and Fort Worth on Tuesday for the follow-up presentation from last week I keep Wednesday open if needed. I decide to go to San Antonio for Thanksgiving, Friday, and Saturday. I can enjoy sightseeing on the Riverwalk, eat some good food, and leave the life-changing past alone for 3 days.

Now time is going fast! The Sunday ritual is the same as it had been forever. Monday the flight to Dallas-Fort Worth is good. No bad weather delays and amazingly no complaints from the travelers. The meeting goes well with the potential client. Somehow I keep missing some points. Either I am slipping or she is really good. I can be ready for a follow-up meeting on Wednesday, but her schedule will not allow it. She is going to New York for the holiday. I book an earlier flight to San Antonio. The weather is unseasonably nice.

What a pleasant surprise! For a change, I am relaxed. I take a tour boat ride down the Riverwalk. As we pass an oncoming boat, the tourists scream out "Kmart shoppers." Whatever that means? I never found out. It must have been something the tour guide put them up to. Thanksgiving Day is relaxing but bittersweet. No hustle and bustle of helping prepare the meal and I certainly don't miss some of the in-laws who were always late for dinner. Since Joann and I were married it has been 5 pm sharp. That having been said, there is a part of me that misses that.

Friday is another beautiful day. Not a cloud in the sky and warmer than normal. I stand in awe in front of the Alamo. Then inside, I take a few moments to pay my respects to the brave people who stayed to the end knowing there was no way out except death. Since I was a child I watched the movies about the battle at the Alamo. The productions on the silver screen did not come close to raising the awareness of what these brave men were fighting for. Standing on that hallowed ground definitely did. It is a nice Friday evening to be out, watching the Christmas lights being turned on, and the downtown storefronts come alive for this special time of the year. Then the thought hits me like a freight train. What am I going to do about Christmas and New Year's Eve?

I arrive back home late Saturday night. "Home" is a strange designation for a place I have only been living in a few weeks. Why fight what it is called? I am only here until I prove the doctors wrong. Sunday morning comes way too soon! I start planning my week.

As I sit at my desk planning the week, I look out the window. The sun is brightly shining, a few puffy clouds in the sky and the birds are singing while looking for food. What a refreshing sixty-second break I have. It is like being in a time warp for me. I forget about work and where I am living.

That having worked so well I changed my afternoon plans. If the birds can sing and eat outside so can I. On the way to the park I stop at a restaurant that the residents of the town rave about the chicken served there. I am not keen on buying chicken at a restaurant. The chicken that I ate came from the kitchens of my mother or Joann. Today I think, "Why not?"

The clerk who takes my order is a young lady probably sixteen or so. She counts my change back to me which is some coins and a ten-dollar bill. Before she closes the cash register drawer, I ask for two, five-dollar bills instead of the ten-dollar bill. There are no fives in the cash drawer so she asks her supervisor to bring to her two; fives for the ten. Curtly her supervisor tells her to give me all one-dollar bills. Instantly I become involved. I want two fives, not ten ones. I press the issue. The supervisor changes her mind, but not her attitude. She brought back two five-dollar bills. After the supervisor leaves, I hand the clerk a five-dollar bill for her tip. Tears well up in her eyes as she says, "Thank you!" She did her job well. It is not her fault the supervisor is poor at public relations skills. Why should I penalize the clerk?

It is a fantastic day to be outside and to enjoy the handiwork of our Creator. It is fun to eat a picnic lunch while I watch the children run and play a few of the many games I used to play as a child growing up. Being from a poor family we invented games to entertain ourselves. We could not afford to buy games. Some of the children nearby are with their grandparents. I know this because amidst the laughter I can hear how they address the adults with them. I reminisce about my happy times with my Grandma and Grandpa Whitford. Since Elizabeth and her family live several miles from me I do not get to visit with them as often as I want due to conflicting schedules. When I get back to the Garden of Eden I will write letters to my granddaughters.

I finish eating my meal. Looking around the park I see a craft fair set up across the parking lot. I go over to browse the booths while being amused by the vendors hawking their wares. There is not a single item here that I need. It becomes a very pleasant, unexpected change of scenery for me.

I walk up to a booth that has miscellaneous items made of wood. There are five or six boxes on the table that resemble recipe cardholders. I stand back and watch as the vendor tries to persuade a teenage girl to open a box. She is afraid of opening a box. The vendor is persistent and pointed to a box explaining to her if she opens the box there is a life lesson in the box. I am intrigued that she is so afraid of what is in the box she will not touch the box with her hand. She relents and uses her cell phone to slide open the lid. When she does she exclaims, "There is nothing in the box! Where is my life lesson?" The vendor smiles and explains, "The life lesson is you are more afraid of what you think is in the box, than what is actually in the box! Do not go through life being afraid of what you think can be, instead of what you know to be!"

After the young lady leaves, I strike up a conversation with the vendor complimenting her on the life lesson she had just taught. I asked her what is in the other boxes? Doing her job as a salesperson she is glad for the opportunity to demonstrate for me. When the box is opened some kind of artificial critter jumps out. A snake, a roach, a mouse, or a spider. Depending on what phobia a person has that opens it makes the difference whether that person laughs or screams. I absolutely am not here to buy a single item, but I buy a box with a mouse in it. I cannot wait for Beth to open it. With that piece of information, I stand at a distance watching people visit her booth opening the boxes. It is more fun added to a delightful day.

The sun is beginning to set. It is such a beautiful sunset. I do not remember ever seeing some of the colors in the sky before. I stand in awe and watch the sun go down. The free show of artwork in the sky is over. I leave the park and go back to the Garden of Eden. Once in my suite, I sit in my recliner gazing at the stars and in my thoughts, I replay the whole day. What a totally wonderful unplanned day it has been.

After relaxing for a few minutes I go to my office and write each of my granddaughters a letter. I take the letters to the lobby and drop them in the mail deposit box. It is not as good as a face to face visit with them. It does show that I am thinking about them and the letters are coming from a loving grandfather. I walk past the dining hall and the retired priest is sitting at a table playing solitaire. I interrupt him. He and I sit and talk about nothing important for an hour. I excuse myself and go to my suite. I set work aside to savor the moments!

I will not leave until Tuesday. This time I am going to the northeast and driving. Being the month of December the weather is iffy at best. I would rather drive and get caught in a storm than to be stuck in an airport trying to get out. Do you know how slow time goes being around the "know-it-alls" that are wiser than air-craft manufacturers and pilots when it comes to flying in bad weather? At least I can get snowed in at a local bar where people are happy to be stuck there!

There's a knock at the door. Upon opening it, there is a smiling, persistent Bethany. I started to give her the same story. Then I thought. She is doing her job consistently and persistently. Those are two of my best qualities. She may be the best friend I can make during my temporary stay here. Beth (Bethany) inquires about my Thanksgiving and the past week. She sits and listens intensely. She grasps every word and asks questions, but nothing personal or about sensitive business information. She is a much better listener than my children. They would only listen long enough to get their surprise from me that I purchased during my trip. As Beth is leaving, she says, "Thanks for taking the time for a conversation." Then she asks, "What are you doing for Christmas?"

"I don't have a clue!" I reply.

Chapter 11
THE "CORNER BAR AND GRILL—MORE THAN A PLACE TO EAT"

"Why am I so intrigued about this place?" I, Charles, ask myself. "Is it the food? Is it the waitress? Is it the owner and how she runs the business? Or is it all of the above?"

During my field trips from the Garden of Eden to the grocery store, the Post Office, and the bank I discover a small family-owned place named The Corner Bar and Grill. It isn't much to look at. The place is clean and the food is good. It doesn't take long to find out the regulars have their reserved seats almost like churchgoers. Heaven help you if you sit in one of their places. This is where many of the locals meet to drink a beer, have a cup or two of coffee, or just pass the time of day while eating a meal.

I get accustomed to all the glares and stares from the self-appointed "seat police." Eating there is pleasant for me. The food is homemade and the service is better! I can sit by myself and reflect on my business trips or life in general. I grade my performance whether it is for my business or my personal life. All of the positives I will write notes on how I can use them more often. The negatives I will address to change or eliminate. Sometimes the answers come while I am sitting at the table. Then there are times when it takes two or three weeks. I always know there is a better way and I am determined to find it. A certain waitress named Lisa catches my attention. By design, I sit in her section.

Over the years I have found that I can learn way more by listening than talking. I am cordial to everyone and at the same time only talking to my favorite waitress Lisa or the busboy. It is amazing what he knows. I guess he is considered a fixture and no one pays attention to what they say while he is nearby doing his job. I do not conduct business in this town so there is not any inside information to be gained. Only the lessons to be learned are how to live and how to treat other human beings. I always leave an extra dollar or two for the tip. That really pays off! I find out what Lisa's schedule is and more times than not I only show up when she is working.

I have the day off and I know Lisa will be working the late shift. I plan to eat there for my evening meal. Off and on during the day while running errands and doing misc. chores a thought keeps coming back to me to give Lisa an extra twenty dollars. To give away twenty dollars will not affect me one way or the other. I keep arguing with myself on the premise that I do not know this person. Certainly, I do not want her to think that I am trying to buy her. I do not want anyone to ever think that of my actions toward them. I cave to my inner voice. That evening after I finish my meal before I leave, I sit at my table and roll up a twenty dollar bill as small as I can. I sheepishly hand it to her on the way out. It will be a week or more before I go back and surely she will forget about it before then. Why am I so nervous about this? I am a tough negotiator and I can sit across the table from the best of them duking it out.

After being out of town, I know, like it or not, I have to go face Lisa. Why did this molehill become a mountain for me? I am seated in Lisa's section. She walks up and greets me with a smile. She does not say a word about the twenty-dollar bill. What a relief that is. The question for me is still the same. "Why am I so nervous about this? Does her opinion of me matter that much?" It is like being in high school all over again! After the crowd leaves, Lisa comes back to my table and the conversation starts off with small talk. Again I am emotionally relieved that none of the words pertain to the twenty-dollar bill. Maybe she did forget. During a return trip to my table, the conversation starts off from her with, "Thank you so much for the extra twenty dollars. You do not know how much that helped me. I needed diapers for my baby and gas for my car. I only had three dollars!" Another life lesson learned for me. Pay more attention to my inner voice.

After this when she sees me walk through the door, she meets me at my table with my drink exactly the way I want it. Then she asks about my day? Most of the other customers have to order their drinks and are greeted with "Do you know what you want to order or do you need more time?" Up until this time, most of my conversations with Lisa have been very limited to small talk like, "Who do you think will win the Stanley Cup?" or "Yesterday it was snowing and today a light jacket will do." Over a short period of time, I find myself growing more and more fond of her. I think there is something special between us. Maybe I should pursue a relationship with her.

I grow tired of eating lunch on Sundays in the dining room at the Garden of Eden so I go to The Corner Bar and Grill. It is a subdued crowd. All of a sudden I hear the volume level of voices escalating. Across the room is a server that I have never seen before telling a man and woman in no uncertain terms to enjoy your free meal and never come back! The man demands to speak to the owner. She replies very sternly, "I am the owner and do not come back!" When things settle down I ask a waitress what is the issue? Her explanation is very simple. The couple comes in every Sunday, always complaining about the food or the service, and the owner has had enough. No one or anything can please them so the owner does not want them around any of the other customers. I think how refreshing it is for the owner to protect her employees. Whether she has one or one hundred, it is her business.

A few weeks later I am sitting in The Corner Bar and Grill one Saturday afternoon after returning from a successful trip. I had finalized a great contract after a long pursuit and a lot of effort! The only thing better than the deal is to be in the company of Lisa. In between her visits to my table, I let my head drift into the ozone layer. Life doesn't seem like it can get any better than this except for the "yo-yo" effect of fighting cancer.

When I am almost finished with my meal, two men in designer suits come in. I do not recognize them. The men do not want a seat. Instead, they motion for Lisa to meet them away from other people. This intrigues me. I want to know who they are so I eavesdrop on them. I can only hear part of the conversation. Between listening and lipreading, I learn they are plain clothes law enforcement officers. Lisa responds, "I do not wait on faces, I wait on tables!" With that answer, the men leave.

I play her answer to them over and over in my mind. I am completely consumed and troubled by it. Am I a face or a table? How can a waitress smile, encourage, answer questions, and be pleasant to a table? I think that is a philosophical question for me to answer when I have nothing else to do! How wrong I am. The question keeps coming back in my thoughts over and over.

Somehow my thoughts get tangled while reminiscing about a waitress at a restaurant in Los Angeles. Taking customers to dinner is like icing on a cake. It is almost as much fun as cashing commission checks. Certainly, there are guidelines, but the evenings at dinner are way more relaxed than the office settings. One particular night I took a customer and her secretary to dinner at an upscale restaurant that I had seen advertisements for, but I had never been to. The food was extraordinary while the service had a major flaw. My guests were very gracious about it. We said our goodbyes and I sat back down at the table.

The waitress brought the check to me. I asked her to sit down. She was surprised, to say the least. I explained that she did a good job of serving my food and drinks, but she insulted my guests. Instantly she wanted to know why I thought that? I took her back through the events of the evening and how every time she came to the table she would ask me what I needed while ignoring my guests. I had to ask her to bring to them what they needed. I explained to her that she is getting a ten percent tip, not because she deserved it, but only because I never leave a penny to be sarcastic. In a New York second, she told me that she knew that I was paying the bill and she intentionally played up to me. In a firm and polite voice I told her that all people are important and if she had waited on my guest as she waited on me, her tip would have been thirty percent!

It is time for me to reel in my thoughts and say "goodbye" to Lisa. I head for home to get ready for next week's travels. I have plenty of time, but I do not like to be rushed if the unexpected happens. Another work week is complete. Why do I keep thinking of the Garden of Eden as home? I am just passing through here!

Time is passing very swiftly. Another week has gone by. Not wanting to sit and eat in the dining room, I decide to go to The Corner Bar and Grill on a Friday night. I find it is a different group of customers from the day or weekend crowds. I receive my regular service from Lisa including the drink, pleasantries, and a big hug with which I totally do not expect, but I am pleased with it. Lisa asks, "Where have you been? I missed you." A short time later, another customer is seated in her section. To my surprise, she walks to his table with a beer and greets him the same as me. Now I am mentally and emotionally totally confused. Does she like me or is it a waitress persona that is hidden until the right two customers show up at the same time? I will come up with a game plan to find out which one I am to her?

While sitting at my table I keep pondering the "face or table" concept! I am very savvy at this game of reading people's motives. After all, that is how I make my money. The amount I make is way above what most people earn. I cannot come up with the answer! I am very aggravated at myself! I do not have the answer that I so desperately want.

While watching Lisa work my mind drifts back to a past business trip to Los Angeles. Not during every business trip do I take customers to dinner. Most of the time my trips are scheduled on a rotating basis. Sometimes my schedule is interrupted because a customer has an emergency break down or an upset condition calling on me for a solution which I gladly provide. During these trips, I will eat dinner alone. This was the case one evening. I walked into a restaurant and the hostess greeted me. She asked, "How many?" Then she quickly explained that the waiting time for a table was one hour. Before I could reply, she told me that I could go to the bar and be seated immediately which I did.

The barmaid was working the bar by herself and keeping up with the customers' requests. Very polite, and not overly friendly, she asked for my drink order and if I wanted a menu? She returned with my drink and a menu. A few minutes later she came back for my food order. The food was good, but the service was excellent! The next day the appointments went well and the day passed by quickly. Not going to dinner with customers I went back to the same restaurant as the night before. I went directly to the bar. As good fortune would have it, the place I sat last night was vacant and the same barmaid was working. She walked over and asked what I wanted to drink? Being in a good mood, teasingly I told her, without naming the items, that I wanted a duplicate order of the drink and food that I had last night. She turned and walked away. I thought to myself, this is going to be interesting.

The barmaid returned with the drink that I wanted. Then I was intrigued and thought she would certainly get the food order wrong. A short time later she brought my food out and it was exactly what and how I wanted it. To say that I was amazed was an understatement. While I ate, I watched her work. She was methodical and never made a mistake. When I was leaving I told her what a great job that she had done and if I was in the food business I would hire her away from her employer. She was very quick to explain that it would not happen. Just as fast I asked "why," I found out that being a barmaid was her way to pay for her education. It was not her vocation in life. She would graduate one month later with an MBA and leave the food industry trade. I thought about the actions of this person many times. She did a better job than most people whose careers are working as a server. What made the difference between her and most of the others? I guess there are many questions, but very few answers!

Chapter 12

CHRISTMAS AND NEW YEAR'S—CHARLES' FAVORITE SEASON

"With my family not living in the area," I ask myself, "what am I going to do to enjoy the holidays?"

From the time I got married, December has always been hectic, but a fun time of the year for me. With the life-changes there will not be the baking of cookies, making candy, treating the carolers to hot chocolate or spiced cider, and preparing the ritual 5 pm Christmas Day meal.

I decide to sit for a while and reminisce about the pleasant times of yesteryears! Shopping for Joann, Elizabeth, and Edward was easy. All of us would take several evenings and go downtown to look at the store windows and of course to see Santa. I would watch Joann as she would pick up a pair of shoes, go back and look at a dress for the second or third time, or stand at the jewelry counter sharing with the clerk how this certain piece would complement this or that. The children would do the same in the toy department. I would follow them through the store. The final decision was always made when the list was verbally given to Santa while getting pictures made. As time went by, Santa went away! But the shopping trips didn't. I would go back to the stores, buy the gifts, have them gift-wrapped, and delivered to the house. Since the divorce and with the children grown, this has changed. I look at the magazines on the plane, pick out the latest gadgets, get on the computer, and have them drop shipped. Some of life is still good.

Baking cookies and making candy was a family affair. We would take one Sunday close to Christmas Day and everyone pitched in to help. It was an all-day affair with lots of fun added. The nice part about the clean-up was the cooking and baking was always scheduled the day before the housekeepers arrived. They were compensated with larger than usual tips and boxes of goodies to take home. I was fascinated by how some humans are conditioned to tips like animals are to food. Then I would try to sort out the difference between commissions and tips. That would always turn into a round-robin, "Which came first, the chicken or the egg?"

It was a treat for the carolers to show up. Joann would invite them in. They would sing two or three carols and would stop to savor the homemade refreshments. Then a few more carols and out the door. They were from a Baptist church close to the house. Reflecting back it seemed as they believed what they were singing about. As they would sing, the countenance on their faces could actually be seen to change, almost to glow!

Back to reality! What to do about Christmas. Elizabeth has had a record year and will be taking her family to a Caribbean Isle for Christmas through New Year's Day for a "Once in a Life-time" trip. She will not admit it, but she did take lessons from her father. I received an email from Edward inviting me to spend the holidays with him, his family, and his in-laws. The jury is still out on that. How many times and how many ways can you dodge the "Where's Joann?" question. Part of the signed divorce decree is to keep my mouth shut. That is hard for a salesperson to do as I laugh out loud!

Enough thinking about the good times of the past and the present-day situation with the family. It is time to get back to running my business. Previous track records show that industrial sales in December are slow. Customers are taking "use it or lose it" vacation days, trying to salvage budgets, or just enjoying the season. For me, after the Thanksgiving weekend, I spend my time sending out hundreds of Christmas cards, having special-made cheesecakes and hams delivered, and the perennial command performances of Christmas parties to attend. Fly here, fly there, drive here, drive there! It doesn't really matter. I enjoy it! It's all part of the business and better than watching insincere TV shows. Christmas is approaching fast!

A few days later Beth stops by to chat. Again she asks about my Christmas plans. She passionately explains that she does not know why I am at the Garden of Eden, but her home and Christmas Day are neutral zones. I think about it for a second or two and then agree.

She is happy and starts to talk about her life which is her family. Then as fast as turning a light on in a room, her face changes as she gleefully shares that there have been some bumps in the road which are becoming less rough and seldom happen anymore. It is interesting that both Beth and her husband are in "fix it" fields.

Beth markets kindness and Hank is the sales manager at an auto parts house. As I think about this, it comes to me that human problems and car problems are both a nuisance. Although it is much easier to get rid of a derelict automobile.

I find a new joy in my heart. Her daughters are 6 and 8 years old. I can make a trip back to town and shop at the department stores. Christmas Day is approaching fast. I find myself doing well financially, mentally, physically and emotionally. Beth stops by and provides directions to her home. It is only about four or five miles from the Garden of Eden. No strict 5 pm dinner. The girls will get up very early to open gifts and the meal will be sometime after noon. This is all strange to me. No structure for sure and along with it absolutely no stress.

Christmas arrives as fast as the north winds and with enough snow to make picture-perfect scenes every direction that I look. I arrive at Beth and Hank's house at about 10:30. The girls are playing with their toys. they are ecstatic to see that this year they are getting a double portion. Beth stops the dinner preparation to watch the girls open their gifts. Dinner is served at 1:37. I happen to look at the clock on the wall. Not 1:30, not 2:00, but 1:37! What a strange time! What is missing are the late in-laws and the stress. What a relief!

It is a great day spent with a true friend and an unpretentious family. What a treat it is to watch the girls play with their new toys! I don't think that I have had this much fun and enjoyed Christmas so much since I was a child living with my parents. I begin to mentally compare how Beth, her present-day life, and her family are parallel paths with my childhood. How hard I worked to get away from the past not realizing what I was giving up to accomplish what I thought was important! It is too late for me. I hope Beth, her family, my daughter, and my son can take the best from my past, and add it to their future, helping them to have a better life. It is a great day for me. I say my goodbyes and head for home.

For years I have taken the week between Christmas and New Year's off. It is impossible to work. Most customers are operating with skeleton crews which over time has proved the best. With some workers recouping from Christmas and the others preparing for New Year's, it does not leave many who want to be bothered with sales calls. I'm off to New Orleans for New Year's festivities. I decide to go two days early to enjoy the food and sights before the amateurs show up. After all of these years of life, I have not grasped the concept of how overindulging, ending up on your hands and knees, puking your guts out in a street gutter is such a great party. Oh well!

I enjoy the trip and New Year's Day is ushered in without incident. The flight home is peaceful. Most travelers are sleeping. Occasionally, someone will ask the attendant for a cure-all from too much partying. It is fun to watch the speed of the service from the attendant. There is a direct correlation between the amount of the mess a person is making and how fast the attendant returns.

Chapter 13

JANUARY—CHARLES SETS THE BUSINESS PACE FOR THE NEW YEAR

"My perpetual New Year's resolution!" I ask myself, "How can I make better use of my time?"

January's business rituals are the same. Naturally this time, the physical surroundings are different. The Garden of Eden is nice, but certainly not like my house. It is hard to believe that I have lived here for a little over two years. During the month of January, in days past I was working in my home office with few or no interruptions. Our children were now adults and had moved out of the house. Joann had become a full-time professor at our alma mater. On nice days, a neighbor or two would drop in and we sat on the sun porch drinking tea or coffee.

Here, at the Garden of Eden, there are way too many people who want me to become part of their lives. I should be flattered. I am way too busy for this. I want to interrupt bingo, take the microphone from the announcer's hand and scream, "I have a life, I don't want another one, leave me alone!" I don't and the urge to do so finally leaves me. Back to business is a top priority in my

77

life. January is a month of strengthening the commitment of my sales staff across the States and part of Canada.

My January travels are completely different now than when I was married to Joann and we were raising our children. I would travel during the week and be home on the weekends. Sometimes I would change my itinerary to be home for special occasions that pertained to the family. Now I leave and complete all of the meetings as scheduled. I travel during weekends if necessary to be more productive and this takes much less time overall. Given the choice, I will gladly go back to my original life. A person has to play the cards they are dealt in life. These are mine and I am making the best of it. I do not like lemons, but nothing compares to lemonade on a hot summer's day!

I finalize the plans to participate in the different charity events across the country. I tried the political dinner circuit, but that only worked well locally. Charity fundraisers are a big hit. All I have to do is contribute enough to be in the top third of the donors. Some places this takes more money than others. Most of it is tax-deductible and the rewards always outweigh the cost. With a little effort, it is easy to get a photograph in their area paper handing a check to the customer's spouse supporting their charity.

Edward invites me down to his house for a visit. This has never happened in January before. He also invites his sister and her family. This is his way to make up for the Christmas get-together that never transpired.

Edward's ideas and goals in life are completely different from any of his family. Not bad, just totally different. He and his wife live in a clean, modest neighborhood a few miles inland from the Gulf Coast. He works part-time for a local landscaping firm. The work is year-round because of building new high rise condos along the beach and the older developments want to stay current with the trends. The rest of his time he spends helping elderly people with their yards, trees, and flowers. His wife volunteers in the gift shop at a hospital in the community. The thought of having children is not even on their radar screen. What a complete opposite from his sister who is married, successfully building her business, and has charming twin girls.

Whose child is he anyway? Did he get switched at birth? He looks like his family! Did an alien take over his body? The good news, he is happy, he is not on drugs and he is providing for his family. His work really adds to the beauty of the entranceways and the grounds of buildings along with the neighborhood. Driving through the area it is easy to see which are Edward's projects versus his competitors! The trip is nice, joyful, and surprisingly no one asks about their mother. Maybe they found out or maybe they decided to leave it alone because the visit is going so well. It is now time to return to the Garden of Eden. I still keep trying to call it home. For some reason, it is not working. Most of my work is complete for the month of January. My customers have closed out the past year and are gearing up for the present.

Totally out of character for me, I start to mix and mingle with some of the residents of Eden. Beth introduces me to a few and some I meet on my own. Meeting people for me is easy. I just pick and choose who they are. After all, it is my life and time. For instance, in the coffee shop one morning I decided to visit with a retired Catholic priest. It starts out as being nosey on my part. Not being religious, but acquainted with it distantly, I am curious to know why he is living at Eden instead of an old priest home. I quickly found out. He is different from most stuffed shirt churchgoers that I had been around. He is passionate about living the life of Christ that he is committed to.

As the priest puts it, "The race is not over. I'm heading down the home stretch." I meet others. The conversations are brief. I get impatient trying to figure out if they suffer from some type of dementia or just living out their last days larger than the life they lived. Either way for me, it is a waste of time. I start seeing more of Beth. She is a pleasant, sincere, and very hard worker. Visiting with her and her family on Christmas Day had made a real soft spot in my heart for them. January is coming to a close. I am ready to get down to the business of meeting with the customers. February is only a week away. That suits me fine. Time to hit the bricks and get going.

Being in sales the marketing plan of the Garden of Eden intrigues me. The strategy is simple; make it where a person can live at different convenience levels. This allows the residents to be from many walks of life and economic groups. The hard part is to make the "well to do" folks always feel "well to do!"

Chapter 14

RELAPSE—AN UNEXPECTED CURVE BALL IN THE GAME OF LIFE FOR CHARLES

"Forgiveness and moving on in life has been a habit of mine forever." I ask myself, "why can I not forgive Butch?"

Sometimes life throws you a curveball. My head is in the ozone on this one. February starts out as planned. I start making my trips again. It is good to see the customers. I think they have cabin fever as much as I do. After about the second week out I seemed to notice a change. I come home tired. It is easier to linger after lunch in the dining room on Sunday than to get started on my tasks. Sometimes out of nowhere comes the thought that maybe the doctors are right. It is easy to dismiss it. I'm getting older. I don't sleep as well. Just like last week! Why on earth did the hotel clerk put me in a room on the floor with a girls' high school basketball team? They were having fun, not doing anything wrong, just being noisy teenagers. I would have gotten more rest next to the ice machine or housekeeping! Maybe my body is not up to the constant traveling anymore. After all, it has been two months since my schedule has been this rigorous.

I decided to slow down a little and see if the slower pace helps. Now fly out on Tuesday and back on Thursday. It seems to be working.

My life as I know it collapses. Not traveling as much isn't working to provide me the energy I want. I decide to go to the doctor a month earlier than my scheduled checkup. I call and change the appointment explaining to the receptionist that I can't seem to beat this tired feeling. I ask Beth if she will trade one of her days off and drive me to the doctor's office. She agrees and refuses to take any pay for the day. That I think is totally different! People not taking money for a service? There is something different about her. I do not tell her that my request for her to go with me is because I am afraid. It is the first time in my life that I am lost. I do not know how to deal with it. The day of the appointment is here and Beth goes with me. The doctors run tests and ask me to wait for the results. I amuse Beth by announcing when you have excellent insurance, you do not have to leave and return for the results.

The receptionist directs me to the consultation room. I ask that Beth is allowed to listen to the diagnosis and prognosis. The doctors then proceed to explain. Like an atomic bomb, it goes off in my head. The cancer that had been in remission has returned with a vengeance. Terminal in 6-8 months. No operation, no treatments, no cure!!!

I have Beth drive me home. How strange it is now: "Home" not the Garden of Eden. The drive takes what seems forever. Beth tries to cheer me up. I think it is partially due to being the sincere good person she is and the other is nervousness on her part. I finally cannot take anymore and yell at her, "If you cannot heal my body, shut up, what good are you?" She starts crying and continues to drive. At home, the Garden of Eden, we part company without saying goodbye. I am very, very angry. Angry at life. Angry at the doctors. Most of all, angry at myself for how I treated a nice person like Beth.

After several hours, I get my act together and decide to drive to Beth's house unannounced. This is one of those screw-ups in life you cannot fix with a telephone call. When I arrive at her house, no one is at home. I know I have to wait. This has to be fixed. When they pull in the drive, I get out of my car. Beth walks right in the house without any acknowledgment. Hank let loose with, "What's the matter with you? Did you not hurt her enough today? Go back to your world and leave us alone!" And with that, he turns and goes into the house before I can say a word. With a very heavy heart, I drive back to the Garden of Eden.

The next morning I choose to eat in the dining room. Depending on my mood or schedule there are some days that I eat there instead of at my place. The food is always good. I can sit, relax, enjoy my meal, and read the morning paper. It is entertaining to watch some of the other residents and what they are doing. At a table over in the corner is where the same two old men play checkers. Depending on who wins the game and the outrage over it, a person would think there is a one-hundred-dollar bill on the line. Some of the women are crocheting. It is amazing to me their perseverance and the detailed patterns they are making. Others just sit and visit. A few people watch television. All in all, like me, they have left most of their past behind and are enjoying or tolerating their present life.

Being tired of the coffee I return to my suite. Sitting in my recliner and looking out the window I start to daydream. For whatever reason, I start to think about Butch. As strange as it sounds I am wondering where he is and how is he doing? Then the question comes to me! As similar as our backgrounds are, how could he and I turn out so different? Statistically, he should have a better, more successful life than me. His father had a better job than my papa. He grew up in a better neighborhood than I did. What is the defining difference?

I drift off to sleep and begin to dream. I wake up startled as if someone in the room is shaking me! Vividly in my mind are images of the homemade tattoos on Butch's hands WHO CARES. Is he constantly asking himself, "Who on this earth really cares about me, what am I doing with my time, or how am I doing in life?" Or maybe, because of low self-esteem, he is telling the people around him with the tattoos he does not care what happens to himself or anyone else. I think about this knowing that I will never have the answer. Only Butch holds the keys to this.

One key that I hold and I do not have the answer. "Why can I not forgive Butch?" I have forgiven Joann and do not have a way to tell her. I know it takes two people to agree to have a mutual affair. I am really struggling with this. In both my business life and personal life I have always been very quick to apologize, ask forgiveness, and to move on whether I was right or wrong. Why not with Butch? I am certain I will never see or talk to him again. All I can do is reach a resolution in my mind about this matter. I have never liked unfinished business. This time this is the best that I can do.

For my life and my success, the answers become clear. I was raised by parents and grandparents who loved me. All of them taught me good morals, good work ethics, and how to interact with people. They gave to me the tools in life to succeed but did not give to me success. For being first and second-generation immigrants to this country I sit here in awe of their insight and how they passed it along to me. For this, I am very, very thankful!

Suddenly there is an unexpected knock at the door. It is Beth. Coldly she asks if the services are acceptable and explains to me that if I need anything, please call the receptionist. Before I can say a word, she leaves. Several days later the same thing happens.

Finally, I catch her alone in the hall and I am afraid. I have not been this way since Beth and I left the doctor's office. She half-heartedly accepts my apology.

In my local travels, the next week, the things I notice the most, are the clerks in the grocery stores and the bank tellers are sincerely friendly. As I think about the irony of this, I cannot come up with the reason why. Both groups provide a necessary service and neither work for tips nor commissions.

In time, Beth softens and painfully tells me how bad I had hurt her! I begin to grow weaker and weaker. The medicine can only control the pain and anxiety. Beth begins spending more time with me. I negotiate a deal with Eden's management to pay part of Beth's salary in exchange for her to help me to finalize the closing affairs of my life. The attorneys have completed all of the legal work for all of my personal estate and my business affairs. Beth's biggest and most important project is to help me complete plans for the great finale of my life: the funeral!

Chapter 15

Charles' Life Lessons Learned—Better Late Than Never

"Since I did not pass all of the life lessons I learned on to Elizabeth and Edward," I ask myself, "should I share them with Beth?"

Beth is spending more time with me! I can tell the condition of my body is deteriorating. We hasten to finalize the funeral arrangements. That is the highest priority.

I want to share with Beth some personal stories. I do not know if I want to do this because I want to pass on my legacy to her or if I think she can learn and make her life better. Maybe both! Many times I wanted to pass these stories on to my children. But we were always too busy.

Elizabeth was into cheerleading, dance, and theater. Edward's time was spent gardening, and participating in science and photography clubs. Joann had her career at the university. I had my business to run to support my family. I always justified in my mind that I was providing for my family—not feeding my ego or proving to Joann's family that I was as rich, as powerful, and as successful as they are!

All of these activities at the time were important or so Joann, Elizabeth, Edward, and I thought. Reflecting back on our life as a family, while gazing out the window, I am sure that most of our choices for what we did were correct at the time. My days left on this Earth are coming to an end. Thinking back into the past there had to be an hour or two here and there that I could have shared my humble beginnings with Elizabeth and Edward doing this so they would know the effort that it took to live the lifestyle that we did.

This being one of my better days I am intrigued by all of these questions that I keep asking myself. The first and foremost question is where do all of these questions come from and why do I care now as I lie here dying? Some of the questions I am able to dismiss and they go away. Other questions will not. This question will not go away and I am pleasantly surprised to think of it when Beth is going to be here with me. She arrives as requested and shuts the door. I hand her a pen and notepad explaining to her that I want her to take some notes.

"Beth, before we start with the note-taking, I have a question for you," I begin. "This question has been plaguing me for some time now. I want a candid answer from you. Does a person need a pure motive to help someone and what happens if the person giving does not?"

Beth ponders my question for a few minutes and then answers me with a question of her own, "What difference does it make about the motive of the giver unless it is obviously superficial or condescending to the recipient? The person or group still receives the benefits. For example, I know you like to be seen and donate at charity events. The people who receive the money or goods still are helped no matter what your objective is. Also, I know that you liked the Christmas carolers and the carols they sang when they stopped by at your previous home. Were they singing for their glory, your enjoyment, or both? All involved were somehow rewarded by their carols. I am sure giving from an unselfish heart is the best, but in almost all of the cases, everyone involved is blessed."

"Back to the original reason that I asked you here. Absolutely under no circumstances is this discussion and the notes from it to be shared with anyone except maybe your husband, Elizabeth, or Edward. I will keep each item brief so you get the message and do not have to take page after page of notes. I was born into a poor second-generation immigrant family who lived in New York City. I was the youngest child. I grew up living in a four-family cold-water flat."

Beth interrupts me, "Charles, you were raised in a four-family apartment building with no hot water?"

"Yes and let me finish, please!" I exclaim and continue. "The apartment on the first floor under ours was converted into a grocery store before we moved in. I learned a lot from my grandpa, papa, and playing on the streets. The biggest lesson that I learned was the determination to leave that lifestyle behind which I did."

She interrupts again. "Charles you have done so well with your life. I always thought you were from an affluent family living on the East coast."

"Thank you, Beth!" I laugh. "You have just affirmed I have reached the goal that I set for myself when I was in the third or fourth grade. Please let me continue. I have more things I want to tell you. You have become like a second daughter to me. What I am sharing with you I have never shared with Elizabeth or Edward. Joann and I were married in the Chapel on the campus of the university."

"You did not have a big church wedding? That is very hard for me to believe!" exclaims Beth.

"No, we did not and here is why. After my mother passed

away, I lost track of all of my relatives. I don't know the reason. Maybe it is because my goals in life are one hundred and eighty degrees opposite of theirs. For whatever the reason, I do not know where they are at or if they are still alive. I regret this deeply. Please do not let this happen to you.

Anyway, back to the church wedding. It was an uphill battle to convince Joann's parents to have it at the chapel. After all, they had the money to host a wedding like the town had never seen. They had been planning this wedding since Joann was old enough to walk. We decided to have a small wedding in a quaint setting because none of my relatives would have been there. I would have had only a few friends from the university and about the same number of acquaintances from my job at the time. It worked well with the open seating. The guests blended together well. Naturally, there were some "old school" people who insisted on sitting on the traditional side for the bride.

Beth, you need to stay in contact with your family. I am not saying to devote all your time visiting but have a family reunion now and then. I know you can't get along with every relative. That is human nature, but be cordial. A friend of mine had a brother who could make a group of nuns angry. He told me, "You can pick your friends, but you cannot pick your relatives!" How true! Be sure you remember that.

Another bit of helpful advice on how to live your life. Years ago I went to a motivational class. After the instructor gave her credentials she asked, 'Does it matter who poisons you?' No one in the class answered her. All of the speakers of this type have to have a "WOW" question. This is so that you will walk out of the class or seminar thinking, 'Wow, why did I not think of that?' I really got my money's worth that day. It was not a trick question. She went on to explain it does not matter who poisons you. You are still dead whether it is your closest relative, your best friend, or your worst enemy. The results are the same. She then related that to personal relationships and people who are constantly negative about life. If they are family, limit your time around them. If they are friends or acquaintances remove them from your life. It may take a while. It can be accomplished!

And Beth last and certainly the most important. When you do a kind deed for someone you may never see the total effect from it. Case in point. When I was attending classes at the university I had to work to pay for my tuition, room, and board. One Saturday I ate breakfast at the cafeteria and went to work. Not having money for lunch, I worked through my break. The workday lasted longer than I had anticipated. When I returned to campus the cafeteria was closed. I wandered around campus passing the time of the evening until it was bedtime. One of my friends happened to pass by and asked if I wanted to go to the local ice cream parlor to get something to eat?

I sheepishly and quietly told him I did not have any money. Without a second of hesitation, he said, 'My treat, I got my tax refund back yesterday.' That single act of kindness toward me is what changed me to start helping people after I graduated. Sometimes it will happen in person. Most of the time it will be through formal organizations. I do not want the recipient to know who I am because I am doing this for them. Of course, some of the plaques hanging on the walls in the university halls have my name on them. I do this so that the current students hopefully learn that it takes many donors to keep the university operating and they will do the same upon graduating."

After finishing this story, I fall asleep and don't wake up until several hours later. Beth is gone. I sincerely want her to grasp what I have shared with her.

Chapter 16

Public Servants—Very Necessary, But Beware Of "Jekyll And Hyde"

"If I would not get involved in peoples' lives who are only acquaintances," I, Charles, ask myself, "how much less stress would I have in my life?"

Beth is so kind to me. It doesn't take a brain surgeon to know life for me as it is now is not near as good as it used to be. Meeting Beth and becoming her friend is like the old, old cliché: "When life hands you lemons, make lemonade." As sure as the sun sets, I would not have traded my good marriage and my good health just to live at the Garden of Eden to meet Beth. Those two items were dealt to me in life. And like a poker hand, I did not choose my cards. But like a poker hand, it is my choice how I play them. I play them to become friends with Beth and she becomes my lemonade.

I am in a silly mood today while Beth is visiting me. For a change, she has plenty of time to sit and chat. I ask her if she knows the difference between a hairstylist, a stripper, a masseuse and a psychologist? With a blank look on her face, all she can say is "No."

I tell her the answer. "A psychologist has a degree and makes more money." She quizzes me on what this is about and where did it come from? With a sparkle in my eye, I admit to her that the main reason that I have been so successful in life is by reading people. I have missed on a few. Mainly the ones I picked on in the joke.

"Let's start with the stylist," I say. "The salon is located in one of the old landmark hotels downtown. The owner of the business is the stylist. He works by appointment only with each service scheduled to start on the hour. This is strange to me. I figured in the course of a day he is losing money because it did not take an hour for each client. I asked him about it. He explained that he did lose money but it gave him time to clean up and every client can walk in knowing that there is no overbooking or waiting. The physical outlay of the salon is nice although unique. It had to have been converted from another use from years gone by. The waiting room is oversized for its purpose. Totally satisfactory, but a waste of space.

To get to the styling room, a person has to walk through an archway and down a very short hallway. No restrooms are needed because this area is adjacent to the old hotel lobby and there are public facilities close by. All of this is strange. Not being an architect I assume it has something to do with the structure of the building. Anyway, one day I am early and he is not finished with the prior appointment. The customer is going through a horrific divorce. The stylist is agreeing with her or making comments that are the exact opposite of what he told me. I thought, *what a racket!* He doesn't have to be responsible for the results of his advice. Beth, at least, you're not like that!"

I am feeling good both mentally and physically. Beth accepts my invitation to lunch. Every now and then our schedules allow for this. When he can, her husband joins us. I haven't been back to their house since Christmas Day. It is always a treat to get to visit with Hank. He is so upbeat about life and very proud of his family. Lunch is over and she takes me back to the Garden of Eden. Beth pulls up to the front entrance and lets me out. She is going to pick up supplies for her office. As I get out, she teasingly says, "Tomorrow I must hear the rest of your story."

The next day after lunch, Beth stops by. I am just waking up from a much-needed nap. She doesn't take time to sit down but as soon as the door closes, she announces that she is here to hear about the stripper.

I say, "I once fell in love with one."

If it had not been for the soundproof walls, the whole Garden of Eden could hear her scream, "You did what? How on earth did Charles Whitford III cross paths with a stripper and fall in love with her?"

"It will be a long story, but here goes," I begin. "One of my customers decided to build a mill on a river out in the middle of nowhere! Out of sight and out of mind was his philosophy. He hired local people to work at the mill, mostly farmers and loggers, known for their outstanding work ethic. For the necessary items to sustain and repair the mill, contracts are awarded to firms like mine. This system has already been established and works well.

Anyway, there is an enterprising bar owner who has a place out of town on the highway going to the mill. He decides to enlarge it and make a strip joint. He changes the name to "Boobies Galore & More." He hires local girls from the surrounding counties. Far enough away most will not be recognized but in tune with what the good old hometown boys want. With this, he knows that most of the money spent will come from vendors and not out of the locals' pockets. Every time before the divorce from Joann, when I was invited to go, I would politely refuse. After all, I was married and true to Joann as she was to me. My papa would have never gone to a place like this and his marriage worked. After the divorce, the next time I am asked to go, I do. It is new to me.

For males and females alike, beauty has always been in the eyes of the beholder. Some of the girls were great, some were ok, and some were oh well. I couldn't help from wondering how they could do that. I don't even like to urinate in front of the same sex. Anyway, the DJ announced a new member of the club would be dancing in five minutes on stage 2. Her name was Angela. Instantly there was a migration to her stage. I remained where I was seated. As she started to dance I watched. What I noticed was she was watching me more than the guys at her stage. The DJ knew how to do his job by building hype to encourage larger tips like a 'ringer' at an auction. Maybe he got a share. I couldn't tell if she was attracted to me or since it was her first night, she made eye contact with me because I was in the safe zone. I bought another round of drinks and left. I had to get to the airport to catch a late-night flight home."

Beth interrupts and tells me that seeing Angela one time was not falling in love. It was falling in lust. For the first time, I sense Beth is a little jealous.

I continue to tell the story to Beth how the relationship progressed over the next several months. "I would show up at the joint before it got crowded. I learned to give the DJ $20 and somehow Angela always danced on the stage by where I was sitting. I noticed her eye contact was with me. She started doing certain things for me and no one else. Naturally, the tips got bigger and bigger. I knew I could outdo the country boys because their wives were not happy about the place and that was why they only had a limited amount to spend without being caught."

Beth cannot wait to hear how it ends and exclaims, "I do not want to hear the details, fast forward to the end!"

"Ok," I comply. "The last time I saw Angela was before I moved into Eden. I chose to stay an extra day so that I did not have to leave and catch a plane. I did this hoping we could meet outside her work. The evening went extremely well! When her shift ended, she got dressed and stopped by my table. Whispering in my ear, she asked, 'Are you ready to leave?' Excited, I did not finish my drink. I took her hand and led her to my car.

When we got to my car she did not want to get in. That was strange, I thought. What would be next? Was she going to give me a sob story for more money? Then I made her promise to tell me the truth no matter how much it would hurt me or whatever it is. She agreed. She started off with the worn-out story you hear over and over. The one where 'it was not easy for me to be a stripper and my husband forced me into it because it was better than filing for bankruptcy.'

I'd heard enough. 'Wait just a minute!' I said while fighting back my emotions. 'Your husband thought! You didn't say anything about a husband when we talked in between shows. You didn't have a wedding ring on and there were no signs of where a ring had been on your finger.'

She instantly speaks up and tells me, 'When I took the job I quit wearing my ring and tanned without it. I knew the attraction and tips would be greater if no one knew I was married.'

I asked, 'So why are you telling me this?'

Angela's reply was, 'I wanted you to know because you are different. The hometown boys would get excited and go home to their wives. The out of towners came in here with their holier than thou attitudes so I gave them what they deserved. A false sense of accomplishment! But somehow you were different. The first night I started working here I saw you. It was a sought after relief from being so afraid and nervous. The natural attraction was there for you from the first moment of eye contact. I focused my attention on you to somehow make-believe it was only you and me. This false sense of security allowed me to continue knowing a divorce was imminent. Then I got hardened to the whistles and catcalls knowing that you liked me. You were a welcome sight.

Accepting your overly generous tips was completely wrong on my part. It was the lesser of the evils of what I faced at home if I did not leave here with the expected amount of money. Do you know how hard it would have been for a 'single girl' to explain bruises to the clientele? There is not a cosmetic made that would coverup bruises without highlighting the obvious. I care deeply for you and I would not leave without telling you that this was my last night. My divorce was final today and I am moving away.'

I pressed for a forwarding address to no avail. The next day during the flight home, I replayed last night over and over in my mind. How or what I could have said to stay in contact with her. With each day, my heart began to heal. To this day, I admire her for the courage it took to tell me and not just leave me not knowing what happened to her! If it is meant to be, she knows she can talk to a mill employee. The good old boys who took me there know all my contact information. They will give it to her just to be nosey to find out what happens next."

All Beth can say is, "Wow!"

Beth's pager then goes off and she has to leave. The next day she drops in. She wants to go outside and learn about the masseuse. I tell her that is not a good idea because the masseuse works here.

"Oh really," whispers Beth. "Maybe we should stay inside." She wants to know which one of the girls it is. At first, I do not want to tell. She pushes for an answer. It would not be fair to the other girl to have a full-blown investigation when only one person is causing a problem. I relent and tell her it is Erika. Emphatically I explain that it is not a problem. It is the extra attention to the off-limit places of my body that makes me feel special. Beth cannot help laughing.

I ask, "What is so funny?"

Then she tells me, "What is funny is that you are neither the first nor will you be the last that gets this special treatment. Management allows it to go on with Erika only for certain chosen residents. Erika makes more from tips than wages and everyone involved is happy."

After Beth leaves. It is lonely for me. I began thinking about some other professions. As you know watching and trying to read people's actions are a large part of my business. "See or be seen" is what I live by and it pays well.

When I traveled by air, whether it was for business or pleasure, I would take taxi cabs as much as possible. If I was calling on a customer or customers that worked in a manufacturing plant or in an industrial complex I would rent a vehicle. When my sales calls were to retail stores or office buildings I enjoyed riding in a taxi. There were numerous benefits for me. Talking to the cabbies was so much fun. I gained a wealth of knowledge from them about what was going on in the local area and sometimes events from around the world. Most of this was dependent on where the cabby was living or had lived.

I saved valuable time because I did not have to check the rental car out, fill up the fuel tank, and check the vehicle back in. Sometimes the lines at the service counter were long, while at other times they were short. One thing was for certain, someone ahead of me in line would have a time-consuming problem to solve. No matter whose fault it was, it took time to resolve it. The cabbies waited their turn in line at the airport and were always available. I did not have to wait for a shuttle to take me back and forth to the car rental lots. Most of the time the cabbies knew the correct route. I enjoyed the ride and asked questions about a variety of subjects or landmarks. I did not have to be concerned about taking short cuts around backed up traffic or finding a parking place. I was especially thankful for this when it was pouring down rain or extremely cold. Looking back on the cab rides I think it was my way to give back to an industry that my papa worked for his entire life and provided money for almost all of my necessities while I was growing up.

Beth returns and we talk about some other jobs dealing with the public one on one. At the bank where I have some of my accounts, there is a lady whose job is a teller. She is well dressed, friendly but professional, and always has a nice smile. On one particular day, I walked up to her window. She was facing away from me. She turned around and had a definite frown on her face. Instantly the frown turned into a smile, not because of who I am, only that I was a customer. From then on I would tease her. Be sure you keep your "customer face" on while you are working.

The local post office clerks were the total opposite of the bank teller. There were three crabby old men who worked at the counter to provide services to the customers. None of the three would smile. I always thought they had daily bets who could frown the worst. I am sure they were in their jobs by seniority. It certainly was not because of their people skills. It was impossible to have everything correct on an item to be mailed. Too much tape! Not enough tape! The address is not in the proper area! The customer being wrong according to the clerks would go on and on and on! I decided to turn it into a game! No matter how bad my day was, I would march in like I owned the place with a large pretentious smile on my face. I would talk too much and would be way overly friendly just to aggravate them. Trips to the post office became much more enjoyable since the three crabby old men retired and have been replaced! The new clerks are pleasant and very helpful to correct any deficiencies without presenting a condescending attitude.

Working at the dentist's office where I was a patient there was a hygienist who was a real "people person." I gave her an "A+" for her patient interaction skills. She had a knack for asking the right questions at the right time about life outside of the office. Eager to have a conversation sometime she would share too much information like "Sorry that I am moody today. It is that time of the month!" Or she might say, "My husband and I were fighting last night because he spent some of our Christmas money at the bar across the street from his job!" Those were issues that I could not help her with and to be honest I did not want to hear about them.

Then one time after my second, six-month interval cleaning, a strange and interesting occurrence happened in the hallway. She had finished cleaning my teeth. We exchanged pleasantries and said our goodbyes. I left the room and went down the hall to the business office. I was about halfway there and discovered that I had left my glasses in her room. I turned around and headed back. We met face to face in the hallway. I greeted her by name. She did not acknowledge me and never slowed down. The light in my brain turned on! All of the conversations were part of an act! She talked to pass the time and divert the attention of the patient from the treatment provided.

Sometime later I go to a different dentist. At first, I was very guarded with my conversations. I was also skeptical about the dentist and his staff's friendly attitude. Afterall I had fallen into the "pretense game" at the previous dentist office. As time went by, I found the present dentist and his staff are as good as their words are. How refreshing that is!

It has been a long tiring day although excellent. I doze off. When I wake up Beth is not here. I start thinking more about the females and males working in the public sector to provide necessary services. Right or wrong, each person has their own actions of getting what they desire! Whether it is bigger tips, a thank you, or mental-emotional fulfillment.

My thoughts drift back to late one night that I was driving home from out in the middle of nowhere. I kept searching for a radio station to listen to hoping it would help me stay awake. I caught the words of a song. "In life's Traveling Road Show, I've been a performer…" I cannot remember any more of the words. It came to me! All of us are performers in our journey! Some are better at our trade than others!

Now my mind is really wondering! It seems to me that every service job requires a certain persona. The big question is what is a false persona and what is the real person behind it? Who knows? Maybe over time the persona and the real person become the same! With that, I fall asleep.

Chapter 17

THE DIVORCE—MORE PAINFUL
THAN DEATH

"Since I am going to die," I, Charles, ask myself, "why could I not have died before the divorce?"

Beth allows me to rest for a day or so. I am on pain medicine and sleep a lot. I know that she stops and checks on me. By now, I have given two keys to her. One to the main door and the other to the fireproof box in the desk and explain that the contents belong to her after I die. I know when she has been here because she always leaves a cheerful note on the table by my bed. The notes are not pretentious or lengthy. Maybe she has taken some lessons from me because she always knows what to write. I can still take care of myself. All my body functions are working normally.

"Please God," I cry, "Let me die with dignity!" Beth comes in and to her surprise, I am awake and rested enough to talk. I start reminiscing about how I met Joann at the university. Then I laugh as I tell her how I became Charles Whitford III. I was not really a third. Not too long after arriving on campus, I realized that I needed to add some flair to my life. I knew I could not lie about my roots for that was too easy to check into. But if I added some pizzazz to my name, people would probably skip over the past right to the present day. It worked well! Talking about my name I have often thought, we are not Whitfords. When I started studying geography and history in grade school, the way Mother and Papa talked and lived did not add to a Whitford heritage for me. I would ask my mother and papa about it from time to time. The answer was always the same, "Son, when you get older, we will tell you all about it." I got older but the answer never came. I don't know if they were embarrassed about the past or were wise enough to propel me into the future. After all, in America, if you dream it, you can make it happen. Enough about the past.

Joann and I were married. Of course, it had to be a proper church wedding. Being a virgin, she looked dazzling in her pure white gown. After a too good to be true honeymoon in the Bahamas, it was back to work. I now had a family to provide for and almost as important was the task of proving to my in-laws that I could cash the check that I had written with my mouth. I am as good as I said I am!

Life is good. Like many newlyweds, we were living in a rented apartment. Before we were ready to buy, a "storybook" house became available in Joann's parents' neighborhood. Joann really wanted this house. It was not the biggest and best house in the old section of town which was still a private community. It was a special house to Joann. She talked and talked about how when she was a child she would ride her bike over to the "dollhouse." I relented and agreed to look at the house with her. As we pulled up to the house I could understand her enthusiasm. I often wished I could have captured the glow on her face while she walked through it. I could not help myself. Her enthusiasm was catching. I had to say, "Yes." As we drove back to our apartment, we were totally excited. Sometimes both of us would talk at the same time. We would stop talking and start laughing like a couple of teenagers. Then reality struck. How could we make the deal?

We agreed, to make it work, help had to come from her parents. We developed a plan which they accepted. It was a loan, not a handout. Joann and I turned the house back into the splendor of yesteryears. One day while in the backyard watching the kids swim a humbling thought occurred to me. Just like the folks sang at the mission so many years ago, "A better day" had arrived. Too bad Mother and Papa had not lived to see it. The home became the center of our lives. I made the den into an office. The children had swimming parties and the dinners that Joann served were second to none for my out of town guests and her university associates.

We had the perfect marriage. Life was good. The children were grown and had moved away. Joann was thrilled to be a professor at our alma mater. Business for me was the best it had ever been. Joann had only two weeks of school left before summer vacation. Summer vacation was nice for her and for me also. She would travel to see Elizabeth or Edward. Some of the time when she was visiting them, I would take some time off and meet her there.

I had been out of town on my weekly ritual business trip. It was one of those weeks where everything fell into place and was completed ahead of schedule. I finished one day early. I didn't call Joann because she was approaching the end of the semester and final exams were coming up. I called the airlines and changed my flight plans. I could leave a day early taking an afternoon flight. The flight would not have been straight through and would have taken about three hours including changing planes.

Upon arriving at the airport, I was informed that all arriving and departing flights have been canceled due to a localized computer virus. The only flight allowed to land is a small express jet with the computer wizards on board. No one could answer the

"How long will it take to fix this?" question. I could rent a car and drive home in 8-10 hours or I could sit in the airport waiting. Even if it was fixed in a reasonable amount of time, would I make my connecting flight?

I decided to rent a car and made the drive. Waiting at the airport had too many uncertain factors. At least driving home I had more control of my destiny. Traffic was moving well. I made good time and arrived home shortly after midnight unexpectedly. My life would never be the same.

The house lights were turned off so I knew Joann was in bed. I left the bags in the car as not to disturb her. I walked quietly through the house. As I approached the bedroom I saw the lights were dim and the door was half-open. I entered the room and what I saw caused a bomb to explode in my head. There was Joann and this guy passed out in our bed. Partially under the sheets, I could see both were totally nude. There were a couple of empty wine bottles on the floor.

At first, I was furious! I thought I should kill them both. No jury would ever convict me! Then when the debris from the exploding bomb in my head stopped falling, I started to think more clearly. If I caused a scene, it would have turned into a "he said-she said" in court. The marriage was over so why not plot to come out the winner. I did not attempt to wake them. I went through his clothes looking for his wallet. I was going to steal his ID. None was to be found. No keys, no money, no wallet. What I did find, I put in my pocket. Four little white pills. I then wrote a note to Joann telling her to hire an attorney. I turned out the lights and left. My life would never be the same! My marriage and home were destroyed.

As I drove down the street I kept burning this guy's face into my memory and the homemade tattoos on his hands. Why did someone disfigure their hands with WHO CARES? As much as it hurt, I vowed to find this guy and ruin his life forever. With a devilish laugh, I knew he would waste his own life.

Then it came down to how I would get even with Joann for this. I drove about an hour out of town and checked into a resort on a lake. Since school was not out, the occupancy rate was down. After three—what seemed to be three eternal days of hell—it was finally Monday. I took the day off, canceled my flight plans for the week, postponed my appointments indefinitely, and called the attorney I have on retainer for the business. She referred me to another attorney because her firm did not handle any type of domestic cases. I immediately started divorce proceedings.

On Tuesday I went to my house and waited for Joann to come home from work. She finally arrived almost three hours later than normal. She was a wreck. Her makeup made a corpse look good. She had been at the park sitting in her car crying. She apologized over and over. All I heard was noise because of the aching in my heart. She wanted me to forgive her for an indiscretion.

"It's not an indiscretion, its adultery!" I screamed. She pleaded with me not to destroy her reputation. I agreed to allow her to stay in the house until the semester was over. She came and went as she pleased. I slept in the guest bedroom. There was no way that I wanted any part of our bedroom or the bed that was in it.

I went to her parents for help. As I went over the past several days in detail, I knew I was breaking their hearts. I could see the agony in their faces. I did not do this to hurt them. I did it to survive. If I would have gone up against Joann, her parents and their attorneys, the emotional and financial drain would have put me back in the apartment above the grocery store in New York City. I worked out a settlement through her parents. Why her parents? They held the purse strings to all of her inheritance. I knew that Joann would not accept a professor's retirement as a way of life. Again, I was right and I kept my finances intact. To close the deal, I shook hands with her father sealing the gentleman's agreement.

As I walked away, he asked one more thing from me, "Please do not ever try to contact her!" As angry as I was, it was easy to pledge that I would not. By now, I am tired and start to doze off. Beth waits for me to wake up. I apologize and ask that the next time she stops by to bring the retired priest with her.

Chapter 18
Charles' Reflections—The Good and Bad

"Why did I wait until I am on my deathbed," I ask myself, "to reflect back on certain issues in my life?"

Two days after Beth's last visit, there is a knock at the door. By now I can just make it to the door. My body is so tired and my spirit is not much better! It is the retired priest. He asks to come in. "Where's Beth?" I ask. He explains that she has been detained at the front desk and will be here shortly. I am glad to see him.

The conversation starts out with small talk as before in the atrium or passing in the hallways. I find it unusual that a priest does not know what to say so I get to the point. I am dying and do not have a heritage in formal religion. I do not know about this life hereafter business. Where do I make the donations? What kind of papers do I need to sign? Do I need to make a list of references to verify the good things that I have done? I can tell from the expression on his face that he knows that I do not have a clue.

He explains that life in eternity is not a business deal. No money! No papers to sign! No witnesses to testify! You cannot hedge your bets. You have to make a commitment from the heart. He asks me to do this. After he leaves, I still don't know what to do.

My commitment to Joann is the only thing I have ever made from my heart. Everything else has been from my head! Thinking back on it, I loved my parents and siblings. I know they loved me, but it was more of a mental commitment because of just surviving.

I can't sit up any longer. The cancer has taken its toll! I lie down. Beth comes in and apologizes for the delay. She wants to leave and come back. Something inside me persuades her to stay. I ask her to stay even if I doze off. Please wait for me to wake up. There are things we have to go over and more things I want to share. She agrees! I ask, "How do I make a commitment from the heart to prepare for and face eternity?"

She explains, "It is really simple. Just pray the words that are in your heart and ask for forgiveness for all of your wrongdoings."

I change the subject. I start discussing the funeral arrangements. She assures me that the church where my former neighborhood Christmas carolers are from will be made available for visitation the day before the funeral from noon until 8:00 pm. The service will be at 1:00 pm the following day with a two-hour visitation preceding. The procession from the church to the cemetery will go through your old neighborhood and by the university.

When it comes to choosing the songs for the service, I am pleasantly surprised that I can remember some songs from the old storefront mission. Once again, she assures me that those songs will not be a problem. She must know a lot more about religion than I do! Thinking about that for a second, I realize that would not take much! I doze off.

When I awake, the first thing I see is her smiling face and she is holding my hand. She has never held my hand. I know she can sense that my end is near. We start talking about the funeral again. Yes, the retired priest from here will speak at the funeral! Yes, the Baptist minister from the church where the carolers attend will speak. Yes everyone on the list will be contacted. Yes, the caterer will change schedules or do whatever to provide the meal after the graveside services. Yes and yes and yes and yes! I tell her I am sorry! This is my last hoorah and it has to be perfect. Charles Whitford III has to go out in style!

I fall asleep again. I look up at the clock when I awake. It is well past Beth's quitting time. She is still here. What a devoted friend she has become. I can hear her on the telephone in the other room telling her husband that she doesn't know what time she will be home. By now they have increased the amount and shortened the intervals between my doses of morphine. She comes back into the bedroom.

I ask her if I ever told her about Butch?

"Who in the world is Butch and why is he so important tonight?" she asked.

I muster the strength and courage to tell her. I start with a question. "Remember the guy I found in bed with my wife?"

She replies with a question, "You mean the one with no keys, no ID, strange tattoos, and only a few pills you stole from him?"

"That's him!" I exclaim. "You would not believe the strange twist of fate that caused our paths to cross. Several months after the divorce, I got back in town late in the evening. There was a traffic backup on the interstate because of a wreck. I decided to take a detour through a part of town I seldom travel. I saw this all-night diner. I was hungry and I went in. Nothing special! Anyway, it looked clean and I was not the only customer. Across the room, I saw a busboy clearing tables. For some reason, he looked familiar.

I got my food and began to eat. I kept searching my mind for where I knew this guy from? No answer. I dismissed it and finished eating. While I was finishing my coffee, he carried a tray of dirty dishes past me. In a New York second, my blood began to boil. On his hands were homemade tattoos—WHO CARES. There is one person on this earth who cares and that is me. I grasped the pointed steak knife in my hand. Something stopped me. I stayed in my seat. I am furious. I sat and made my plans. I started going back occasionally and made it a point to befriend the different waitresses and the busboy. I would listen to their stories and not tell them mine. When the busboy wasn't there, I found out his name was Butch and the neighborhood he lived in.

I hired a private eye. After a few weeks, the PI has the information I wanted. As I read the report, I started to feel sorry for Butch. His life started out similar to mine. His dad was elderly when he was born. Maybe he was a "mistake." His brother and sister are much older than he is. He was essentially an only child. Growing up the big difference was his parents owned a small home. His dad worked at the local mill and made a decent living. He lived by himself in an apartment above his parents' detached garage. And most of all, he was living a life not knowing "who cares?" While the PI did his work, I did mine. I would go to the diner. When Butch wasn't there, I sat and read the paper while I listened to the waitresses as they talked. When things were slow, their conversations turned personal. It was as if I was invisible. There was no limit to what they said or who they gossiped about!

The more they talked to each other, the more I found out that Butch, the laid-back guy had used them all. To their amazement, he had sex with all of them. And they had fallen for the century-old lines! Distraught over losing a girlfriend, having a hard time figuring out his sexual orientation, and the biggest one was being a misfit that nobody cared for.

At the last meeting with the PI, I thanked him for doing a good job and left him with this thought: "It will be worse for Butch not to know his demise than to know what it will be!" He looked puzzled as I paid him and walked out the door. Several nights later I went to the diner when Butch was working. I paid my check and tipped the waitress. After a trip to the restroom, I walked back by my table before it was cleared off. Discreetly I left the four little pills I had stolen out of Butch's pocket and a note with a small mirror. The note read: 'Carry this mirror with you so you do not have to turn around constantly to see who is following you and what your demise is going to be.'

As I drove home, a huge question loomed in my mind. Why Joann, why? And why with a common busboy especially an average looking busboy who is a deadbeat!"

I sob as Beth is holding my hand. I know I am going to die without knowing the answer. Beth is silent for a while. Then asks, "What became of Butch?"

With a gleam in my eye, I grip her hand and by now I'm having trouble knowing the difference between what are conscious thoughts and dreams. Being a "control freak," my biggest concern about dying is that I have no control over what happens in the next life! I have all these questions that no one can answer. One of them is, what will we do with all the time we have? After all, eternity is a very long, long time.

Another thought that will not leave me is why I did not have the intestinal fortitude to ask Lisa the waitress if I was a "face or a table?" That was completely out of character for me. After all, I was a success in life enticing people to bare their souls to me. When they did, I was in control of the situations. I would then play on their sympathy or go for the jugular. With her, why couldn't I ask? Does she mean that much to me and I am afraid of what the answer will be? Or is she the perfect "imaginary" lover and my ego will not allow anything else? Oh well! I'm too close to death for it to be a concern now!

Then my mind drifts back to Joann. I never stopped loving her. Why didn't I forgive her? Why didn't I try to work things out? Was it that I was "old school?" Or was it that her parents helped decide our fate and they are "old school." Some things that happen in life are forgiven, but certainly not forgotten! I now realize I have forgiven her. I have just not forgotten what she did. With much regret, it is too late for me to tell her. To my dissatisfaction, I will die not knowing the answer to one of the most important questions of my life!!!

I regain my senses. I give a half-hearted chuckle. She laughs too when she found out the next day after I left the pills, Butch quit his job and took a bus to Atlanta, Miami or some point south. WHO CARES Butch was nervous and evasive about his destination when he left. Butch never knew how I found him and in his mind, he will always wonder when I am going to show up again. That is his demise. I start to drift in and out of consciousness. I know I need to say "goodbye" to Beth. Neither of us knows this will be the last time we will see each other while I am alive. My pain is getting worse. I call for more and more morphine. Being terminal, the nurse relaxes the rules about the doses. In between hits, my mind constantly recalls the meetings at the storefront mission and the words of the Christmas carols from the carolers. I decide to commit my heart and my mind to the great Creator and Architect of the Universe!

Chapter 19
THE FUNERAL—THE GRAND FINALE
OR IS IT?

Beth receives the call during the night that Charles has passed away. It was a short night. She drives to the Garden of Eden rehearsing in her thoughts what she will have to do. The coroner has already been called. No autopsy is required because of the situation. The attorneys are notified and on their way.

The coroner gives the approval to remove the body. The attorneys swoop in and remove the computer and business files while Beth watches. She signs a receipt for the items taken from the suite and keeps a copy for the office files. She now makes the unpleasant call to notify Elizabeth. After the call is made, Beth removes the bedsheets, Charles' dirty clothes and towels sending them to the laundry. She closes and locks the door while taking the fireproof box with her. She hides the box in her office. She promised Charles she will not open it until after the funeral.

She calls every person on the list that Charles had named! It is quite an ordeal. When the last few names are called, it is as if she was a machine. It is like press 1 if you will attend. Press 2 if you will not attend. Press 3 if you will be eating lunch at the church hall afterward. Press 4 if you need directions. Press 5 if you need help finding lodging. What a day! The next few days will not be any better.

Edward receives the inevitable telephone call from his sister. "Elizabeth tells me, 'Our father has passed away.' From conversations with my sister I know Beth was very kind to keep her updated on our father's condition and that he had made almost all of the funeral arrangements. Beth explained, "Your father did not want to burden you with this." We laughed and agreed it was mainly because he wanted it done his way and that is his excuse! Daily, Elizabeth and I had mentally prepared for this call knowing that it would happen. The unknown was when? Still, it was not emotionally easy to hear those words from my sister.

At the arranged time, Beth meets Elizabeth and Edward at the Garden of Eden. Together they ride to the funeral home and finalize the arrangements. Charles made all of what he thought to be important decisions including the guest list that reads like a Who's Who, the service, and the food. Elizabeth and Edward have to pick out the casket, the clothes, and the flowers.

Knowing it is a sensitive subject from her conversations with Charles, Beth asks, "How is Joann and where is she living?"

Edward, with agony in his voice, relays to Beth the long conversation with his grandparents and how a consensus was finally reached about telling Mother. To Beth's amazement, Joann will attend the funeral. The arrangements are finished. Every "I" has been dotted and every "T" has been crossed. It is almost eerie as if Charles is present to make sure his departure is being orchestrated in the grandeur required for a big-screen production.

I, Joann, ask myself, "I have to go to the funeral for Charles. Will I be shunned or accepted?"

I board a plane in Paris and head to the States. If there are no glitches with the flight I will make it to the church a few minutes before the service starts. During the flight home, I keep struggling with what to expect? How will I be treated? Who knows what I did? Not having the answers I order a double scotch and water. After I finish the second drink, I fall asleep.

The flight attendants are serving our final meal before we land. After eating my meal I begin to reminisce about Charles. Maybe the passing of time or the excitement of Paris has dulled the memories of the busboy. Somehow in my mind, I always thought that Charles and I would get back together. It was like we were separated and not divorced. I know that he loved me! He never dated anyone after our divorce! He worked just as hard at his business as if he was providing for his family and impressing mine!

It was like being hit by a bus when my father called me and told me that Charles had passed away. Now here I am a widow. My mind drifts to the busboy. I am trying to think of his name. Butch, that's it. If I should happen to see him while I am at home, I will make sure he does not have a big head because of the affair. Did I use the word "affair?" I meant indiscretion! In no uncertain terms, he will know that his head will be deflated like a blow-up doll! I fall asleep until the plane's wheels touch the runway. The cab ride to the church seems like it takes forever.

There is a constant line of people going through for the visitation before the service. The ushers do a good job of seating people. It is more like a wedding than a funeral. The church is filled to capacity. Standing room only! I am seated by an usher. It is a seat in the middle of a group of people I do not know. I do not have any idea who they are or where they are from?

The service starts on time, with the old hymns, and just like Charles is there in person. The Minister reads the obituary. During the obit, are oohs and aahs from the people in the audience.

Then comes the silence as quiet as a church mouse when the words are spoken, "Survived by my friend and the mother of my children, Joann."

When the minister finishes with the preliminaries the priest from the Garden of Eden speaks about living, dying, and eternal life. It takes me by surprise that Charles has a Catholic priest preach his funeral. I did not know that Charles even knew a priest. I will find out more about this.

The words of his homily are very exact about life choices a person makes for life now and for the hereafter. Then he delivers the life lesson. The priest tells a story about a visit to a friend who is an undertaker. As he sat in his friend's office at the funeral home he saw two jars that looked identical on the desk. His friend asked him to pick up the jars and tell him what the difference was between the two. The priest goes on to say that after looking the jars over carefully that he could not see anything different. His friend complimented him on his observation that there was no difference. The jars held the cremated remains of two men. The defining difference was when the two men were alive. One jar held the remains of a poor farmer who barely kept his family fed working hard at it and was kind to everyone. In the other jar were the remains of a greedy old man who cheated everyone he could including his mother. Now both of their remains in jars were sitting on the desk as equals!

Suddenly the thought hits me hard. What have I done with my life and what am I going to do with the rest of it? These thoughts play over and over in my mind. I am oblivious to the rest of the service.

I am brought back to reality by the usher dismissing us to walk past the casket for the final time. After I get my head out of the ozone I hear the words being sung by the soloist of the closing song. It is "Silent Night." Charles' all-time favorite Christmas carol. Even though it is out of season, there is no surprise here because Charles always marched to a different drum. I am sure that Charles is having a "holy night." As I walk past Elizabeth and Edward I sense they are relieved that they did not have to give eulogies. When I look over the audience I am amazed that none of Charles' relatives are here.

What an affair the funeral was! It was a lengthy service. Almost like what the pope or the president would have. The procession to the cemetery through the town is a parade with police escorts. Many people who do not know Charles watch from the sidewalks as we drive down the streets. Some are watching the funeral procession out of curiosity because of hearing it is the "Must" attend event of the year, while others want to say they are a part of it. We pass by our old home and go by the university. Charles was very proud of graduating from there and continued to be an active part of it.

The townspeople continue to talk about it for several days. Mostly flattering comments! A few think it was a waste of money. The most common phrase spoken is: "This town has not seen a funeral like this since that politician died! By the way, what was her name?" Then the debates start all over again. Nothing is ever decided. It does get the participants out of their winter doldrums!

Chapter 20

THE FUNERAL LUNCHEON—CHARLES WOULD HAVE ENJOYED IT

"Knowing my father made out the guest list," I, Elizabeth, ask myself, "where are his relatives?"

The graveside service is short and everyone goes back to the church hall except Joann. What a fanfare the luncheon is. The only thing missing is the band like the Titanic had. The stories are never-ending about Charles.

At one table they are talking about the cars he would drive to call on customers. One person is telling how Charles would never drive anything less than a luxury car. Charles would never miss a chance to proclaim this was the reward of working hard and should be an incentive for everyone to do the same. At the same table, the next guest told of how she never saw him in anything but a compact. Charles' philosophy was that you had to be frugal to stay alive in the tough economic times.

The next table was talking about Charles' business clothes. About the tailored suits and the monogrammed shirts. "You have to be kidding!" one of Charles' newest customers exclaimed. "He always showed up in jeans and a work shirt touting the phrase, 'you can't make it in this world if you can't crawl in the holes with the workers doing their jobs.'"

Table after table, the message becomes clear. It does not matter whether it was about vacations, dinners, gifts or whatever. The guests realized that none of them really knew more than one facet of Charles' life. The attendees looking back at him saw Charles was to every customer what that particular customer needed him to be. No more—no less!

As I am mingling with the guests going from table to table a woman approaches me and introduces herself and asks, "Elizabeth, do you care if I go to the podium and tell a story about your father that I want everyone to hear?"

"You may and thank you for asking," I reply.

The woman goes to the podium and turns the microphone on. She introduces herself and explains that she is a single parent and carpools to work to save money. Continuing on, she speaks of one day Charles was in her office making a sales call. She received a call from her teenage daughter's school that her daughter was sick and needed to go home. As soon as I hung up the phone, Charles was instantly aware something was wrong. He asked, 'what is the matter?'

"When I shared my problem with him," she says, "he immediately handed his car keys to me explaining his afternoon was filled with appointments in the plant." She goes further by telling the guests that Charles sincerely enjoyed helping people. "He did not cater to a certain group of customers who could award him contracts more than to the ones who couldn't. He did not help customers just to make a sale."

As she finished her complimentary words, three more people were waiting at the podium to speak. I did not get there in time to stop them.

An elderly lady spoke softly and precisely with tears in her eyes explaining she does not know Mr. Whitford. She tells the story of how her path in life crossed his several years ago in a grocery store where she had to ride a city bus to go there. She started to pay the clerk and her money was missing from her purse. She looked and looked. The money was not to be found. She was going to leave her groceries, go get the money, and then go back to the store for her items. The gentleman behind her motioned to the clerk he would cover it. She wanted his name but he would not give it out. She never saw him again until she saw his obituary and picture in the paper and cannot let this go until her final respects are paid.

As I regain my composure, a couple in their twenties begin to tell their story about my father. It was funny and at the same time refreshing because she will start to say something and he will correct her or vice versa. It is cute watching them because I can see they adore each other, making sure the story is told correctly. They brought to my memory, visions of how my parents looked at each other years ago. The guests at the tables stop eating and talking to listen to the couple. As with the elderly lady they did not know my father. They, too, saw his obit in the paper and came to pay their respects.

When they were teenagers they were in a candy store on Valentine's Day. He had chosen some candy for her and they were in the checkout line. Either the candy was mismarked or he miscounted his change. He did not have the money to pay for all of it. Trying to be good to his girlfriend at the time, he asked her to choose which candy she wanted? Before she made a choice, both in unison told about this gentleman at the back of the line asking the clerk, "How much is the young man short?" Thirty-nine cents was the answer. The man paid the thirty-nine cents. This man they did not know helped make their Valentine's Day special.

His wife (girlfriend at the time) had Valentine's Day candy and he learned there were still caring people in the world.

With that, the stories at the tables start up again. Many of the people linger around. Who knows how long they will stay if the minister does not dismiss them so the custodians can clean the hall. As the guests are leaving there is a consensus reached that Charles sold to his customers what they needed, not what they wanted, at a fair price along with excellent service! As emotionally hard as it is, but certainly gratifying, I and the rest of my mother's family learned about the many facets of my father's life we did not know. I wish that my mother would have attended the luncheon. Maybe she did not want to answer any questions about why she went away and where she has been? Another nagging question in my mind as I walk out of the hall, "Why didn't any of my father's relatives attend the visitation, the service, or the luncheon?" I was introduced to the guests before the meal was served and thanked everyone for attending. The guests know who I am and not one person introduced themself as a relative of my father.

Chapter 21
JOANN—REVISITING THE PAST

I spend the afternoon and evening driving around in my rental car. Things haven't changed much.

As I drive around, I keep asking myself, "Why do I keep letting that worm of a man (Butch) keep controlling my life? I am the person with the money and the education. Why am I not controlling his life?"

I know that I am driving around to pass the time since I am afraid to face the guests and answer questions at the funeral luncheon.

I stop in front of our old house for several minutes. Then I drive to the park where it took three hours for me to get enough courage to face Charles to apologize and ask for his forgiveness. Nagging thoughts keep occurring in my head about Butch and the waitresses. I will go to The Majestic and walk in as if I had never been there.

After staring into space for an unknown amount of time I leave for The Majestic. Somehow I make a wrong turn. Determined to go to the diner I turn this way and that way to correct my mistake. As I am about to give up, there is the root beer stand that Charles, Elizabeth, Edward, and I would go to almost every Friday evening during the summer. Now I know where I am at. It will be easy to get to The Majestic from here. I have plenty of time so I pull in the parking lot and stop. It is closed for the winter season. I sit and think about how many good times we had here. No matter how tired Charles was from a trip, this was a must-do thing and he never complained. It was a family thing to do. His only requirement was that everyone had to drink their homemade root beer. Eat what you want, but this a root beer stand. Enough reminiscing, I have to take care of business at The Majestic.

Arriving at the diner I park in the lot. As I peer through the windows, I see that the entire crew has changed. No Butch and all the waitresses are new. I decide to drive to Butch's apartment. In my mind, I know it will gain me naught. My ego keeps telling me, he has to understand how insignificant he is. When I arrive at his place, there are no lights and a "For sale" sign in the front yard. By now, my curiosity is getting the best of me. I drive back to the all-night diner and go in. I order a coffee for the continuous refills and a meal that has to be served in courses. I do this to buy time at the table. After some time and a little small talk with the waitress, I ask if she knows "A busboy who used to work here named Butch?"

She laughs and says, "No. I have only heard stories about him from some of the other waitresses before they quit."

I lay a twenty-dollar bill on the table with the understanding she will repeat what she knows as she has time. I pay my check in case she gets busy. When she comes back the first time, she tells me that Butch is dumb "like a fox."

"What do you mean?" I ask. It is the farthest thing from my mind that WHO CARES Butch is smart. Again she laughs and before she leaves my table she whispers that he was having sex with all the waitresses using pitiable, poor-me stories. "Amazing," I tell her. I sit there and drink more coffee. When most of the customers leave, she comes and sits at my table.

She exclaims that she has saved the best story for last. "It is a hard story to believe, but no one can dispute it," she begins. "The story goes that a local female professor from the university started coming in here with some of her students. That she was intrigued with Butch and started talking to him. One night after she left, the waitresses began teasing him. They told him 'don't get too stirred up or you will have to go home and take care of yourself.' Butch counteroffered with a five-dollar bet with each of them that he could have sex with her. In unison, they all wanted in on the bet."

"Did Butch win?" I ask.

"Whether it is true or not," she says, "they forfeited the money because several months later in the local paper courts section there was a divorce notice and she left town."

I feel a knot growing in my stomach. The waitress leaves and waits on other customers. When she has time and comes back, I ask, "What happened to Butch?"

She begins to tell me and starts chuckling out loud. "That is the funniest part of the story. The rich bitch's husband hired a private investigator and found out who Butch is? The husband must have been cold and calculating."

"Why's that?" I ask.

She responds, "Instead of storming in here and making a scene, the guy came in and ate a meal. When he left, he placed four little white pills, a mirror, and a note on the table where he had been sitting. When Butch came to clean the table and saw the pills, he turned pale as a ghost."

I tell her while the story sounds good, she has not answered me where Butch is at?

"Nobody knows for sure. When he quit, he showed a bus ticket to Atlanta or someplace south."

Instantly, I become nauseated. I hurried outside where I threw up. WHO CARES Butch was a spoiled user. I came face to face with reality. I was a twenty-dollar bet. Butch used me. I had not used him!

Chapter 22

SPRINGTIME—BETH'S NEW BEGINNING

"Knowing Spring is a renewal time for this planet we call Earth," I ask myself, "will I be included?"

Elizabeth and Edward have been spending time with friends and family. Their grandparents agree to allow Joann to return from her exile in Paris. As sad as it is, Charles is a late husband, not an "ex." Joann is now a widow. Elizabeth and Edward have two haunting tasks to do before they say their goodbyes and leave town for their homes. They have to remove a few of their dad's possessions from the Garden of Eden and attend a prearranged meeting with their late father's lawyer to settle his estate.

It is bittersweet! Elizabeth asks Edward, "Do you know how hard this would be if Father was living at our old house when he passed away?" No response from Edward, only tears in his eyes. They meet Beth at the appointed time. It was already decided Elizabeth and Edward will only take three cardboard boxes. Nothing else really matters to them. Beth helps them take the items to their vehicle and after saying goodbye, Beth goes back to what was Charles' suite.

I decide to keep some things for memory's sake. The rest I

take to the cafeteria. There is a table in the corner of the room for such items. It is like a bargain basement for shoppers except the items are first come, first served and are free. Once in a while, there is a dispute between residents over a treasure. Most of the time it is resolved when a cafeteria worker threatens to throw the treasure away and bar the "kids" from the table for a month.

Returning from the cafeteria I take the fireproof box back to Suite 111 from my office. It now has become 111 instead of the Charles Whitford III residence. At first, I hesitate to open the box. Who knows why? It cannot contain any bad news! I have already completed all of Charles' requests. His children are grown so no deathbed promises about them. I open the box. One lone envelope with my name on it in Charles' handwriting. When I pick it up, I know there cannot be much in it. I slowly open the envelope. A small handwritten note reads: "Dear Beth, This is the name and telephone number of a local attorney who is handling my estate. Because of the urgency of my business, a Trust has been set up. The meeting will take place two days after my funeral. In the Trust, you are listed as a 1/3 beneficiary of the money I leave. None of the business. Elizabeth inherits it." It is signed, "Charles Whitford III. P.S.: And thank you for being such an unselfish friend!!! With that, I place the unlocked, empty box on a closet shelf."

I go sit on the bed, emotionally overwhelmed, and tears well up in my eyes. I read the note over and over and over again. Although there is no amount specified, I know it is more money than I have. There's a knock on the door. Not expecting anyone, I go and open the door. It is a coworker and I invite her in. The coworker sees the tears in my eyes, and tries to console me saying "That's so sad about Charles." Without any sign of emotion on my face or in my voice, I reply, "Not really. It is probably for the best. You know I was starting to like him." With that, remorse hits me like a piano falling from a window five stories up!

When I gain control of my thoughts I crawl out from under the make-believe piano that fell on me! Being paged my coworker leaves the room without saying a word. I rush over and close the door locking it behind her. I fall across the bed weeping out of control for what seems like an eternity. I am soaked from tears and so is the bed! I have never cried like this in all of my life, never ever! Charles was always good to me and my family. Friendly, but not one time did he make advances toward me. He was very self-sufficient. I did not have to humor him. Now he is gone forever!

How selfish can I be? How can I change or do I really want to change? If so, how do I become what I want to be? Why am I so afraid of change? Where can I go to get the help that I want and need? This is way too much to ponder about today. Surely, I will think about this again, maybe tomorrow.

Then my brain begins to spin questioning, Who will be the next "Charles"? How soon will he or she come into my life and then go out of it like Charles? Will this cause me to change for the better or the worse? I pick up the envelope placing it out of sight in my pocket. I then look around and there is one of Charles' favorite plaques still hanging on the wall "TODAY is yesterday's TOMORROW! Get it Done!" How could I have missed taking that off of the wall? Removing the plaque, I turn out the lights, shut the door, and lock it.

I take my purse and go to the ladies' room. Without looking in a mirror I know my face looks like nine miles of muddy road. The reflection in the mirror validates my thoughts. As I wash my face and apply fresh makeup I keep replaying the events of this afternoon specifically and my relationship with Charles. Some more tears and some more makeup repairs. With my emotions finally under control, I go to my office.

I call my husband and explain that I will be an hour or so late.

Hank is not concerned. I have been detained at work before. Calling is a courtesy I always extend to him and he does the same for me. I keep going back to the words that I spoke to my coworker about my relationship with Charles. I bounce my thoughts back and forth about the words out of my mouth. Where did those words come from? I keep reflecting on how good Charles was to me.

As I pass the receptionist I inform her that I am leaving early and I will be on vacation for the next week and a half. I drive to the park instead of going straight home. I sit in my car. My thoughts go back to the first time I met Charles. In the beginning, he was strictly business. It took a while but cautiously he began to share with me what was in his heart and mind. Why did I keep this self-created defense mechanism from many years ago in place? I thought I was over that a long time ago. Undoubtedly not! I have never let this interfere with my relationships with my parents, with my dear husband Hank, with his parents, and with our daughters. Why Charles? How did I hide this from Charles and more importantly, how did I hide it from myself?

I start crying again. I was brought back to reality by a police officer tapping on the window. I lower the window. She greets me with a smile and asks if I am ok? Yes, I am, I think! A close friend recently passed away. A close friend and in reality he certainly was. Why did it take so long to admit this? This afternoon I had to distribute the last of his personal items. I realized he is gone forever. Upon hearing what happened the officer left allowing me to grieve. Again I look in the mirror. What a mess I see and more make up repairs.

I go home to Hank and the security of being held in his arms. I tell him about the events of the whole afternoon except the words I spoke to the coworker about Charles. I keep this from him and I do not know why? Am I afraid that he will love me less? Am I afraid of speaking the words and hearing them again will reveal to him and me what I have been hiding from? Am I afraid of the truth? I vow to myself somehow I will find out and resolve this issue. Not today for I am finding the comfort that I need being held in his arms and I need it so much! I asks myself, "How hard-hearted am I?"

Chapter 23

THE JOURNAL—CHARLES' UNREVEALED LIFE

"After all of the stories we heard about our father at the funeral luncheon," Elizabeth asks Edward, "what else is there that we do not know about him?"

It is going to be a long quiet drive back to the hotel where we are staying from the Garden of Eden. The funeral was yesterday. The next order of business is meeting with the attorney tomorrow which was prearranged by our father. This will not be mentally or emotionally easy for Edward and me. But you know Father, no procrastinating! His motto was "Get it done and out of the way!" The numbing effects of our emotions are slowly wearing off. It is sinking in dramatically that he is no longer with us on this earth!

All we have now are the great memories and the dark cloud that hovers over because of the divorce. No one will explain to us what happened and why our mother suddenly moved to Paris, France. She is too old to be pregnant! There is some small talk that Mother wants to study art and become an artist. Who knows, maybe she is reliving her childhood? One thing is for certain is that we will probably never find out.

Curiosity is building constantly about the contents in the

boxes as Edward and I are driving back to the hotel. Like it or not we agree to open the boxes after our 10 o'clock appointment tomorrow with the attorney. We need to be on top of our game for this meeting and neither of us wants to make any more decisions today.

Edward and I arrive at the law office a few minutes ahead of time. Much to our surprise, Beth is there. She greets us cordially. Certainly not with the warmth that was extended to us yesterday for whatever reason! The attorney is straight forward without any fanfare. The meeting is very short. She explains our father's assets had been placed in a Trust which had been witnessed and recorded. There are no physical belongings to dispose of. When your father was pronounced "terminal" he created a list of who gets what and that is my responsibility to see it is carried out. All of his liquid assets have been located and placed in one account for easy transparent distribution according to the terms of the Trust. All of his personal property at the Garden of Eden has been distributed as per his request. There are no outstanding debts. Money will be placed in an escrow account for one year to satisfy any claims. All of the liquid assets will be divided equally between Elizabeth, Edward, and Beth. The business in its entirety now belongs to Elizabeth. "Seed" money has been left in the account to operate the business for six months. Your father was a great man! This meeting is over.

Back at the hotel room Edward and I begin to go through the boxes one at a time. The first box contains mostly photos and mementos. The photos are family pictures. Some photos neither one of us have seen before. Pictures of our father's family. People we do not know or have even heard of! We are pleasantly surprised when we find on the backs of the photos, names, dates, and how we are related.

The second box contains legal papers about the business, contact names and numbers. Copies of filed income tax forms.

Mother and Father always filed "separately." We never knew why? Maybe it was what the accountants wanted or maybe it was because Mother was from "old money!" In our society, old money and new money never mix!

Opening the third box causes instant curiosity. In it, are two objects wrapped in old yellowed newspapers bound with frayed twine. Edward and I are intrigued by it. Before he and I could open it, we started asking each other questions. Was this the object that our father had hid in his office that we got a glimpse of one day in passing? When we peeped through the doorway he would not explain anything about it. He politely asked us to leave and to close the door. We gently untie the twine and remove the papers. Wrapped in the papers is a very old, well-worn jewelry box. We discovered it had belonged to our grandmother (our father's mother). On the inside of the top of the box is a love note written to her from our grandfather. Then scribbled on a small piece of paper is a note from our grandfather with the date he finished the box and how he selected each piece of wood especially for her to make the box! How special!

After taking a few deep breaths to calm our emotions we begin to remove the items one at a time from the box. We look at each piece. There is a wedding ring and a broach that belonged to our grandmother. Grandfather's gold wire-rim glasses and his union card. The card is well worn and tattered. It revealed he was a proud union member showing it to many people!

Facedown is a photo that when turned over shows a picture of our parents on their wedding day with his wedding ring taped to it! We then realized he loved our mother until his last breath was taken and his heart stopped beating. If only he had known how to repair the damage? The truth be known our mother probably still loves him too!

The next item in the box is a hardbound journal with numerous opened postmarked envelopes held in place by crumbling rubber bands. It has been a couple of years since the envelopes or the book had been looked at. Both of us thought here are the keys to the divorce. We will finally know! In it are entries revealing a man, our father, that neither one of us knew. Not a list of women's names and numbers or contacts who owed him favors. It was entry after entry of places he had donated money or supplies to and he never breathed a word about this to a soul!

Of course, we went to church on the important traditional holidays—Christmas and Easter. He gave money to us to put in the offering plate along with him. During the Christmas season, while shopping, he never passed a red kettle without dropping some money in each one of them. Page after page listing the agencies, addresses, and telephone numbers where his donations went. Some were for foster care. Some were for shelters for single mothers and abused women. Some went to churches to help families have a better Christmas. The largest and most continuous was to his alma mater. He had a special fund set up to help students through an unexpected financial crisis. At his directive, no person was to know who he was. Most of the agencies required that the recipient write a thank you note that was mailed to our father by the agency.

As I pick up the bundle of letters, Edward and I both notice the letter at the bottom of the stack is not nearly as discolored as the rest.

Edward and I agree to look at the letters starting at the top just in case there is a significance in the order they are placed. We will open the cigar box last. Both of us know how meticulous our father was with his filing system. After looking at each letter we are down to the last one. To our amazement, it was never sent through the mail and it is addressed to Edward and me. What could it be? With much anxiety, I open the letter and start reading it out loud.

To my dear children, Elizabeth and Edward,

Time has passed way too fast! I cannot believe that both of you are young adults and have your own journey in life now. When you were teenagers I wanted to share these thoughts from my heart with you, but for some reason, it did not happen. It always seemed when I was emotionally ready our time together got diverted because of the doorbell or telephone ringing, dinner was being served, or it was time to go to some event. So I am writing this letter to you while in a hotel room during a business trip.

From the time that your mother told me the good news on two different occasions that she was pregnant until this very day, there is great joy and love in my heart for you! While you were growing up we had an excellent life! I did my best to be there for the important things. Now I realize what was important to me may not have been important to you! I am so sorry that I did not ask you what event you wanted me to attend? I traveled because of my business, but I could have changed my schedule if you wanted me to.

I know there were some rough times. No family is perfect! I can't remember very many. Some people will say that this is denial. As many bad times as I had growing up, I tried to address the issues that pertained to you and move on with life! If for some reason, there are things that are bothering you, please share them with me so that I can make amends. This will allow you to forgive me and all of us can go forward in a positive manner.

Do you remember the great vacations that we went on? How your mother, you, and I sat at the dining room table on a Sunday evening, two months ahead of time making our plans? We would take two weeks every year and go someplace different, coast to coast, border to border. Everywhere we went was exciting! From the Empire State Building to Niagara Falls. From the Great Lakes to the vast fields of grain in the Midwest. From the Grand Canyon to the Redwood Forest in California. From Graceland in Memphis down to the French Quarters in New Orleans. Watching the space launches in Florida and then up to Washington D.C. There are too many other places to mention. But for me, the most hallowed places were to stand on the grounds of Arlington National Cemetery, Gettysburg National Cemetery, to walk through the Alamo, and to pay my respects at some of the other National Cemeteries! These men and women served our country so that we can be free! I know our country is not perfect. I hope you can grasp what it has taken for us to get this far and purpose in your minds to make it an even better place for all! I know you cannot help every person you meet, but you can help some along the way. That is the most important.

I planned to mail this letter in the morning when I went through the hotel lobby. I suddenly realized what I wanted to share with you was a face to face conversation so the discussion would be going both ways between the three of us. The conversation did not happen nor was this letter mailed!

I am so sorry that I did not have the courage to share these thoughts with you. I believe it was because when I was growing up times were very hard! Emotions were kept to ourselves. We were in survival mode! I was taught not to add to someone else's burdens. Please forgive me for all of my faults and shortcomings!

With all my love,

Your Father

Edward and I cannot stop the tears. We look at each other and are speechless!

In every letter from the recipients were heartwarming words of how the money or the supplies made a huge difference in their lives when it was needed the most. A few follow-up letters shared some encouraging words from him. This journal and the letters exposed a hidden life of our father that we were clueless about! He would watch the evening news and complain about all of the people who were asking for handouts! Edward and I agree he must have done his homework, donating money where it was truly needed and would be used wisely. This proves to us that a person cannot be judged solely on the lack of visible actions and no one really knows what is in their heart.

There is also a very old cigar box. Looking at the printed words and magazine pictures glued on the outside of the box we knew it had to belong to our father when he was a young child. It was his treasure chest for his keepsakes.

Edward and I are apprehensive about opening the "treasure chest." After all, we are riding an emotional roller coaster like neither one of us has ever ridden before. We have absolutely no outside support to help us through this except each other. To our surprise when we open it, the flood of tears is here again. In the box with a few old coins is his Cub Scout knife along with all of the homemade valentines that Edward and I made for him over the years. Both of us knew that he kept them on his desk for the month of February. After the holiday was over, as children, we thought he threw them away. And then the emotional trip started again. Under the valentines were love letters from our mother to our father. Not many. Only enough to show us she loved him until the end. Undoubtedly he loved her or he would not have saved her letters. Edward and I ask each other, "Why did she leave? Why did they get a divorce?" Maybe someday we'll know!

In a few weeks hopefully, Edward and I can sit down and truly grasp what Father was telling us, what he expected us to do in the future, and how much he dearly loved us! After a very long and exhausting day, we decide to part company and go to bed.

The next morning we meet for lunch before going back to our homes. Over and over we laugh at finding the many unknown facets of the life of our dad we had come to know over the past week. This is one hundred and eighty degrees different from the chilly stern father we were raised by. Could it be he guided us the way he did while we were growing up so we would succeed in life? Then after his death, he showed us how to really live by helping others and not asking anything in return. The two hours at the table goes by too fast! I become the keeper of the box of treasures wrapped in the same newspaper and bound with the same frayed twine. Only the memories are allowed to escape! We say our goodbyes and Edward drives away first. I start walking to my car. The realization comes to me hard and fast that like it or not, I am thrust into my dad's business!

Chapter 24
BETH—A CHANGED PERSON

"Why did it take so long for me to forgive Charles?" I ask myself. "If he did not have a place in my heart why did his angry words hurt me so much?"

After Charles' death, my life at the Garden of Eden has changed dramatically. I took some much-needed time off to rest and to catch up on the needs of my family. With much thankfulness, I admire how my husband and daughters understand about the time it took away from them and the amount of mental stress it was for me to be a caregiver for Charles!

Upon my return to work, I am informed that my job scope and duties have changed. I will no longer care for patients. My new position is to develop and be the director of the marketing division of the business. This has nothing to do with the relationship I had with Charles. I am told that the owners discreetly observed me while doing their monthly tours. They were impressed by how I could answer the questions from residents as well as from the visitors. I am given an office adjacent to the lobby providing easy access for guests and the media. The sky's the limit! I set my goal to raise the occupancy level to 100%. The rate now, which is acceptable, varies between 80 and 85%. Why not work hard and smart to make it 100%? When the meeting is adjourned I go directly to Suite 111, previously where Charles resided, to make a final walkthrough.

It has been rented to an elderly lady. It will be cleaned, new carpet installed and painted with her colors of choice. I look in every corner and run my hands across the shelves located in the closets. On the shelf in the room that was his office, I find three unopened envelopes that are addressed to Charles. Two of them have return addresses for charities here in our city. The other return address is from out of state. Automatically I call Elizabeth. She instructs me to open them. I find in all three, receipts for donations stapled to letters of appreciation and gratefulness! After collecting my thoughts I am surprised and in awe that Charles donated to any charities. Elizabeth explained so was she and Edward when they opened one of the cardboard boxes. It contained letter after letter revealing the same thing. During all of my talks with Charles, he never hinted of donating anything to anyone. Elizabeth requested that I mail the letters to her so she can keep them together.

Elizabeth and I chat for a few minutes and say our goodbyes. I sit down on the carpet in a corner. It is like being in a "time warp." Charles is gone and so are his personal belongings and his furniture. I lean back against the wall and close my eyes. I daydream about how good Charles was to my family and me. He did the unthinkable for us.

Totally unexpected, but very much appreciated, the money from Charles could not have been received at a better time! It was almost like Charles himself planned it this way. The owner of the auto parts store where my husband works wants to retire. None of his children want to follow in their father's footsteps and take over running the business. The owner and Hank work out a deal.

They complete the terms of the sale with the guidance of the attorney that did the legal work for Charles. I was happy with this because I know I can trust her and I know the fees charged will be fair. I have enough money to make the required down payment and still have a sizable amount left over. The extra money will be a cushion for the months when the sales are lower than anticipated. Oh, how I wish Charles could be here to guide us through this sudden change in our lives, an opportunity of a lifetime journey. This is an added blessing to our family because both of the girls are in school. I can drop them off at school in the morning. They can ride the bus to the store in the afternoon. While they are at the store they can dust or sweep and ride home with their dad. This will be an excellent learning experience for them. Getting paid a small amount will allow them to buy some extra items while feeling good about their accomplishments. I know from life the best gift, other than love, parents can give to a child is to plant and help the child build true self-worth!

The pleasant daydream is over. I do not want to leave the room. From out of nowhere and who knows why I start speaking in an audible voice just like Charles is in the room with me. Charles, if you can hear me: thank you so much from the bottom of my heart. And I forgive you for the day that you screamed at me. Your words, the tone of your voice, and the volume at which the words were delivered hurt me so bad! Now you will never know how much! If you would have plunged a butcher knife into my stomach the pain would not have been worse. I am sorry that you are not alive to hear me say all of this! As I finished speaking these words and listening to what I said, I cannot believe what a relief there is. Why did I not do this earlier?

I just learned what Charles had practiced for years. As soon as he spoke those hurtful words to me, he asked for forgiveness. He did his part. I did not do my part until now. How good I feel.

This event has given to me the determination to rid myself of the lifelong building of emotional walls to keep certain people out of my life.

The passing of time has allowed me to heal and realize you were not mad at me. You were angry at yourself. For the first time in your adult life, you were facing something you knew you could not fix! The mental and emotional stress that your time on this earth will run out before you can repair your broken marriage to Joann was taking its toll! May you rest in peace Charles!!!

Chapter 25
JOANN—RETURNS TO THE STATES

During the trip home, I ask myself, "How am I going to adapt to my new, old way of life?"

As soon as I find out my "exile" has been terminated I ask my parents to lease an apartment for me close to their villa. As good fortune would have it, they find one. I am sure there are no sidewalk cafes. I will miss the Parisian way of life I have come to love so much. I am on a plane again going back to Paris. I don't think I have rested from the flight to the States two weeks ago for the funeral. I don't know how Charles did it. He traveled weekly to service his customers and never complained. The departure is delayed by some type of electrical malfunction of the conveyor that loads our baggage on the plane so I fall asleep.

I am jolted awake by the plane leaving the gate. This time to my amazement my sleep has been peaceful. Is it because my family is allowing me to return from exile? Or is it because Charles has passed away completing that chapter in my life? Whatever it is, it is pleasant not to have those recurring negative thoughts. Even though I did not hear it from his lips I know in my heart that he had forgiven me. I kept wanting us to resolve the issue that caused our divorce and start over. It never did and now it will never happen for sure! The stress is slowly leaving, but not the memories. Now there is absolutely nothing that I can do about it.

The skies are clear and the weather is good. The pilot announces, "Ladies and gentlemen, sit back and relax. I am anticipating a quiet and uneventful flight. If all goes well, I plan to make up for the late departure and to touch down in Paris on time!" It really doesn't matter to me what time I get to Paris. I have already alerted housekeeping of my arrival and for sure my apartment will be freshened up for my return. The housekeeper is very good at her niche in life. My residence sparkles from one end to the other after she has been here. She brings fresh cut flowers for each vase in every room causing a nice sweet natural fragrance.

I begin to write a list of people that I want to visit, things that I want to do, and places that I want to see before I leave Paris for the final time unless it will be to visit. Just like a switch turning off a light, I fall asleep.

Several hours later the flight attendant awakens me as she serves us our meals. Following lunch, I go back to working on my "To do" list. I thought it would be short and simple. The list keeps growing longer and longer. A must-see place is the Palace of Versailles.

The plane arrives on schedule and late at night. It was a smooth and uneventful flight which was good for me after this past week! It is too late for me to ask any of my friends to pick me up. I take a taxi and the city lights are so beautiful. I will definitely miss my new friends along with the view of the skyline. Opening the door to my apartment is beyond my expectations. Everything is in its place, and yes there are the fresh cut flowers! Although being tired from the trip I will unpack and put things away.

For the first time since I have been living in Paris, tomorrow certainly will be a "new" day! No more double Scotch and water drinks for me tonight to dull the pain as in the past. Living again in America will be bittersweet. Two totally different lives I have lived. The new life in Paris has far fewer responsibilities and I like that. The only time that I need a clock or a calendar is to go to my scheduled art class or meet friends at a prearranged time and place for lunch or dinner. Meeting for breakfast has never been on my "radar screen." I do not want any early morning obligations. When I get back, I will have the self-appointed opportunity to help take care of my aging parents and renew my relationship with my daughter and my son. Recently my sister and her family have moved to the West Coast.

Once I get back to the States and settle in, I have one more item of business to complete. What am I going to do to and about the "worm" (Butch)? The reality is that Charles punished him more than I ever could. That was a trait very few people saw in Charles. He certainly knew how to get even, but because of the way he lived his life, he very seldom used it! I wonder if Charles reached a resolution with this before he died? I question if Butch knows about his passing? If Butch does, I ponder the thought if he will return home from his self-imposed exile? Emotionally I start preparing for the battle when I see him. Then I calm down as rational thoughts travel through my head. How do I know where he is at? How do I know if I will ever see him? How do I know if he is still alive? Why am I plotting and scheming for an event that may never happen? With those thoughts, I fall fast asleep.

Dawn comes way too fast! I wake up more rested and refreshed than I have for ages. Casually I walk down to my favorite sidewalk cafe for a late breakfast. I can sit, eat, and finish my "To Do" list in a leisurely process.

My final days in Paris pass in a blur. I complete my art classes on schedule. The art instructor, with his connections, schedules two field trips to Art Hill. We actually set up our easels and paint. What a thrill to sit and paint on Art Hill thinking about some of the masters who sat here and painted before us. I am satisfied with my paintings. Some of them will go back with me while others will be left to be sold. The proceeds will go to help a talented student who does not have the funds to complete the entire course.

I book my flight arrangements to go home. Home, what a strange but welcome word to me. My life in Paris is coming to a close and the next passage in my life is about to begin. I have said my goodbyes. Dinners with friends are finished. I made my last tour boat ride on the River Seine, went up in the Eiffel Tower, and sat on a pew in Notre Dame Church giving thanks. I spent a day walking through the Palace of Versailles and touring the grounds. What an eye-opener! The palace is light years ahead of my family's home. And I thought I grew up in an "upscale" neighborhood!

All of the packing of my personal items are complete. Thanks to the kindness of the housekeeper she will have the other items shipped to my new address. She has always adored my "designer" purses so secretly I packed all of them in a box. I gave the box to her on the condition it will not be opened until after I leave. I know you cannot spend "purses" so I also placed some money in the box. I certainly hope she knows how much I appreciate her. I learned this from Charles. Growing up I watched the hired hands get paid a wage for performing a task, no more, no less. The way Charles grew up was to reward people for performing above and beyond what was required. I like his way much better!

Of the four Transatlantic flights back and forth to Paris, this will be the best. I am going home!

Chapter 26
Edward—Planting New Seeds

"Without my father to guide me," I ask myself, "what will I do?"

Information going from one person to another person in our family travels at different speeds. The news that I received today was hoped for a long, long time. It came via an unexpected call from my sister Elizabeth. The words did my heart good. What a great dose of medicine for my soul. "Mother is moving back to the States and will arrive in our old hometown tonight!" Other than my wife Monica who is now pregnant with our first child and my family, being emotionally attached to someone has never been my thing. Probably to the extroverts, this would seem to be some kind of disorder. It has worked for me. The pregnancy was planned and to both of our delights, it happened quickly. Now with Mother returning, I will renew our relationship. She can visit and be a grandmother to our child. Monica and I have plenty of room in our new home. It is not newly constructed, only new to us. It took a lot of work, sweat, and tears to restore it to the grandeur of days gone by. Our place even has a "mother-in-law" cottage. How charming is that?

The house and property are from the estate of a wealthy owner of a chain of grocery stores. It was exactly what we were looking for. There is plenty of room to grow plants with a medium-sized greenhouse. I found out that the previous owner loved nature and plants as much as I do.

We now live farther inland from the Gulf of Mexico. The soil here is rich and fertile, not like the sand on the beach. Basically, the only things that grow in the sand are sea oats and some kind of scrub brush. Having my own greenhouse is a childhood dream come true. I can work on my research projects and not have to commute to the company campus. Best of all I can grow a wide variety of flowers year-round for my wife.

Our father was always proud of Elizabeth and me. He was pleased to find out about Monica and our new home. We talked about it as much as we could during the last few phone calls. When he was at his weakest the calls would only last three or four minutes. He never failed to ask how Monica is doing and then about me. The final question was "What projects around the house are you working on?" After I would answer his reply would be, "Don't ever forget that I love you son and I have been forever proud of you!" Those were the last words that I heard him speak to me. How precious is that?

Mother has arrived for a two or three-week visit. Monica and I are so thrilled. I have looked forward to this for such a long time. First, Mother was gone from my life for some not-to-be-discussed reason. Then, Father passed away. Without my wife, I would have been an orphan. Not knowing how long Mother and I are going to visit, at midnight, Monica goes to bed. Mother and I stay up until 2 a.m. talking about everything and everybody except her leaving and my father. Something deep inside of me wants that to be part of the conversation, but I will not bring it up.

Up bright and early the next morning after breakfast we drive to the Gulf to show Mother the white sandy beaches and to take a tour of a quaint little town. She falls in love with the people, the shops, and the restaurants. Certainly not near the variety of shops as in some of the larger cities farther away. It is a simple thirty-minute drive from our house. Most of the buildings in the town are fairly new. Somehow Mother Nature with the use of the hurricanes sees to that! There are three old buildings that have stood against the test of time and the destructive forces of the storms. All three of the buildings need facelifts, but like their owners, have been here longer than anyone else in town. An old-style gas station, a fish market that sells the daily catch, and a storefront Gospel Mission. Each one serves its purpose.

The gas station has a couple of well-worn benches out in front where the old-timers come and sit on nice days, whittle with their pocketknives, and tell larger than life stories. All of this happens while the owner pumps the gas, washes the car windows, checks the engine oil, and the air pressure in the tires. The first time that I saw this it reminded me of a scene from an old black and white movie. Can you imagine sitting and watching an entire movie without any color? All of my life it has been self-service gas pumps at convenience stores.

After a few trips with us, Mother gains the confidence to drive herself to the beach. She knows the town is safe to walk around in. Listening to her talk I am sure it reminds her somewhat of Paris although not near as glamorous.

Chapter 27
JOANN VS. BUTCH—WHO IS THE WINNER???

"Too many times to count since the divorce," I Joann, ask myself, "if and when I meet face to face with Butch, how will I get even with him for all of the grief he has caused my family and me?"

One day Monica and Edward are busy with appointments so I (Joann) have the day to myself. I decide to drive to the beach and walk around the town. While looking for a particular boutique I walk by the old Gospel Mission. It is a chilly, but not a cold day. There is a beggar sitting on the mission steps asking for money. He is clean and so are his ragged clothes. His hair and beard need to be trimmed in the worst way. He is wearing gloves. He is so thin physically I can almost see his cheekbones. Definitely an illegal drug user or alcohol problem I think. Maybe both! I toss a crumpled up five-dollar bill in his plate. I did not want him to see what it was until after I was gone. "Thank you!" he politely said. I keep walking.

During the quiet drive back to Monica's and Edward's house

I keep thinking how familiar that voice sounded. I dismiss it from my thoughts. Until I went with my son and his wife, I had never been in that town. No one I know is that destitute.

Two or three days later I go back. It is much warmer today and the sun is shining. I go and walk on the beach first. The sand is cold. I tolerate the chill for how good it feels squishing between my toes and massaging the bottoms of my bare feet. I walk up the beach and then go back to my starting point. I sit for a while observing the seagulls beg for food and the dolphins play in the waves. I look at all of the footprints in the sand among the shells, jellyfish, and driftwood. If I was a writer I would write a book, "Footprints in the Sand: If they could talk, what a story they would tell!" With that, I go to the outdoor water station, rinse off my feet, and put my shoes on.

I deliberately walk to the mission to see if the scrawny old man is there. Where do I know that voice from? Maybe the voice is from a movie or a commercial? Or is it from a record or a radio personality?

There is a man sitting on the steps. From a distance, it appears it is the old man that was there several days ago. As I get closer I know it is him. He is wearing the same ragged clothes. This time he is not wearing any gloves and I see the faded homemade tattoos on his hands that read WHO CARES. Instantly I am sick, very sick and ready to vomit. I have found Butch without even trying. Somehow I keep my composure and toss a five-dollar bill in his plate. Again, politely he says, "Thank you!" I hurry away out of sight of everyone. I go in an alley. I vomit and vomit and vomit so much that my rib cage is hurting. I clean myself up and go to my car as fast as I can.

All the way back to Monica's and Edward's house I begin to plot my revenge and how sweet it will be! It took Butch and me together to perform the acts that we did, but now it is all his fault. I, Joann Whitford will make him pay dearly for what we did!

Out of nowhere, a thought comes to me. Take a lesson from your late husband Charles. It worked so well for him and it will work for me. Take your time and plan out your actions.

Everything is settled in my mind and my body somewhat calmed down by the time Monica and Edward return home. As we are eating dinner I ask if I can stay for another two weeks. Both, instantly, wholeheartedly agree.

Now I will have to wait for an opportunity to go by myself and confront Butch. A week later it happens. I go straight to the beach and park about a block away from the Mission. I can see a person sitting on the steps and I hope with all of my being it is Butch. I am walking slowly rehearsing my speech all the way. All of a sudden I mentally ask myself "If forgave myself, and I know God forgave me, why can't I forgive Butch?" The answer did not come to me. Butch is there! I may never have this opportunity again and I will not pass it up. I know that I am going to carry out my plan of revenge. Right, wrong, or indifferent!

As I walk up to him, he says, "Hello!" with a smile. I toss four little white pills in his plate. The blood drains from his face as he gets up and starts to run. Little did I know all of the training that I did while being a cheerleader and a performer years ago would come out suddenly and give me the ability to take the enemy down.

Being in better shape than he is physically I trip him. He lands on the broken concrete sidewalk hands and face first. He starts to get up but I jump on the middle of his back holding him down. He desperately tries to get up with no avail. His years of hard living have taken a toll on him. I grab him by the hair on his head. I speak softly but sternly in his ear explaining he is a nobody. Always has been and always will be!

He starts crying while telling me that he was conceived by a mistake and that was well known.

"I was born because my mom and dad did not believe in

abortions," he continues. "I grew up knowing no one cared for me. That is the reason for the poorly homemade tattoos on my hands that read WHO CARES. All of my life I have been seeking to find someone who cares and that person has never shown up. When I got the job at The Majestic I learned to take a nobody and turn myself into somebody in my very, very small world."

I let him get up. At this point, I am also shedding tears. I ask him to forgive me for harboring such revengeful hate in my heart against him. He apologizes for all of the harm he has caused me and accepts my apology. I give him a quick friendly hug telling him to walk through the door into the mission.

"When you get inside, bow your head and ask for forgiveness from the Supreme Creator of the Universe," I tell him. "He will forgive you and His love is unconditional. To grasp this, read and believe John 3:16 'For God so loved the world…'"

With this, I tell him that we will probably never see each other again and wish him the best of luck. With a smile, he says, "Goodbye!" Then he picks up his plate and hurries toward the door into the mission.

As he is walking away, I tell him, "By the way, Charles passed away because of cancer." I don't think he heard me. He didn't turn around or acknowledge what I said.

What he does inside the mission I will never know. He may walk straight through and out the back door. That is solely up to him. By now a crowd begins to gather. Not wanting any questions I slip away. I leave in a hurry. The tears have made a mess of my makeup and especially the mascara. On the way to Monica's and Edward's house, I stop at the Visitor's Center. I repair the makeup and brush the dirt off of my clothes. If I don't, this will be tough to explain. I am absolutely not ready to discuss the divorce.

In a few days, I will regretfully return home. This is a totally different trip than I planned. The good news: two more items from the past wiped completely off of the slate. Renewing my relationship with my son and his family is at the top of the list. Not too far behind was closing the chapter of Butch in my life. I think both Butch and I are pleased.

Chapter 28

Elizabeth—Distribution Of Wealth

"Am I ready?" I ask myself. "Am I capable of following in my father's footsteps?"

Driving home from the funeral I take the interstate. It takes about an hour longer. The sky is blue, not a cloud in the sky, and the sun is shining brightly. What a magnificent day to cruise the open road. It is the beginning of the week. There are not many vehicles on the road. For sure I miss my husband, Darin, and our twin girls Jamie and Joanie. He deeply regretted that he could not attend my father's funeral. This is not an issue with me.

Darin is the president of his union. Their contract is about to expire and negotiations are long and tedious. None of the talks are shared with me other than he tells me what his best guess for when he will be home. I know he wants to make the best deal he can for the members while not putting the owners in jeopardy of going bankrupt or out of business.

I chose this route to drive home because I need time to think and sort out the occurrences of this past week. No loose ends to tie up from the funeral or from my late father's estate which is a huge blessing. I learned over the years he paid attention to the

161

details. No surprise here. Both went well. Not one small glitch with either nor is there anything left to do, except I am now the owner of his business which is far larger than mine. It has more employees and covers a vast amount of the United States and part of Canada. What to do? This is the only purpose for the longer drive home.

Without a doubt, both of the businesses are running like well-oiled machines. It is because of his hard work and likewise the same for me that this is the result. I turn the radio off so that I can concentrate more on how I am operating my business and what my dad did to make his business successful. My thoughts go back and forth while I brainstorm.

In another mile or so there is a rest area. I will stop there and put my thoughts on paper. I park in a spot at the very end. This is working well. Occasionally a bird will fly by. I have my notebook out and start writing. On the first page is how I run my business and changes that I can make in order to spend less time at the office. The only change that I need to make is to hire a manager. Loyalty, trustworthy, and dependable are the "must-have" qualifications along with a state broker's license for Insurance and real estate sales.

Next is how to play the cards dealt to me on how to run my late father's business. This is a challenge. I know he has customers in numerous states from the East Coast to the West Coast. From Florida and into Canada. First and most importantly I have a family that I dearly love and want to spend quality time with them. Secondly, I have an established business that I built from the ground up and I will not sacrifice it. I ponder these thoughts and ask myself, "What would my father do?" With no answer on the horizon of my mind, I start driving home.

The rest of the drive is short and uneventful. Turning down our lane the answer was clear. Taking a lesson from his journal and letters in the box, he would have brokered a deal with the suppliers and sold off some of the territories to his sales representatives in designated locations. How does brokering a deal with the suppliers relate to the journal and the letters? The words in some of the letters revealed how my dad helped some people not only for one instance but also for a lifetime. There is an old Chinese proverb. "Give a person a fish and you feed that person for a day. Teach a person to fish and you feed that person for life!"

I hurriedly got out of my car. Darin and the girls are so excited to see me. They are waiting on the sidewalk by the drive. After hugs and kisses, Darin wants to carry all the items in the house for me. "Please not now. What I want more than anything is to sit down and visit with you and the girls." I did carry a single box in and head straight to my bedroom. This made all of them curious beyond belief!

What a treat it is to be home with my family. The next morning I get down to the tasks of unraveling two businesses and re-weaving them into something that will work for me, my family, my customers, the sales staff, the suppliers, and will definitely be a success. And in that order exactly. I know that this is the correct direction to go and dad would not accept anything less.

First things first. I write an advertisement to run in the "Help Wanted" section of the local paper and drop it off on the way to my office. In between telephone calls, I plan the next steps of running my new business. That really sounds strange to me. All of my entire life it has been my father's business. Given time I will get used to it.

The decision is made. I will retrieve the list of contact names and numbers from the box. Taking the list of customers, suppliers, and sales personnel with me to the office the next day I start methodically laying out the new territory lines. Many of the names are familiar to me from meeting people at the visitation and funeral for my dad. I can put a face with some of the names while others I cannot. I call each person on the list explaining that in two or three weeks I will start making appointments so that I can meet with each one of them face to face in a business setting. This will speed up the learning curve to provide the best service possible.

Meanwhile, the ad in the classified section attracts more attention and replies than I ever expected. I begin sorting the resumes sent to me as fast as they come in. I have high hopes that one of my three choices will accept the job and will be the manager that I want and need. I call the three applicants and set appointments for the interviews for the day after tomorrow.

Following a nice dinner at home, I make the announcement that I have a treasure left to me from my dad and I want to share it with them. Darin and the girls immediately move to the living room. This normally does not happen this fast. All of us participate in clearing the table, rinsing the dishes and starting the dishwasher, and putting the leftovers in the fridge before leaving the kitchen.

I go to my closet and return with the boxes wrapped in the old newspapers and bound with the frayed twine. In unison, they ask, "How old are these?" Carefully as before, I unwrap the jewelry box. All eyes are fixed upon it. Question number one is "What is it?" I answer their questions. Next, I open the box letting Darin and the girls hold each piece while I explain the significance of it. Upon seeing the treasure chest the girls know what it is! They have boxes of their own. The old coins and the scout knife did not fascinate them, but looking at the valentines did! The last question is "Why is there a journal and letters hidden in this box?" The mystery unfolds and Darin is lost for words. Humbly he admits that this is a side of his father-in-law that he never saw. I confess, neither did Edward or I. The girls are too young to understand all of this.

With that, I take the boxes, the newspapers, and the twine to my bedroom. I hesitate for a minute or two before I begin to wrap things up. I leave the journal and the letters out. I carefully secured the jewelry box and treasure chest with the twine and newspapers that had been used for many years. Placing the boxes on my closet shelf I am pleased that I decided to keep the journal and letters in a place that is easily accessible for reference and guidance when required.

The interviews go extremely well. It is a tough decision. I choose Jill, candidate number two. She is a single parent born and raised in this town. She is prompt and very articulate with her answers. Courteous and directly to the point. No "poor me" stories. I hire her. Her first day is Monday. She is on vacation so that works well for her two-week notice. I set aside a week to train her and that is more than sufficient. She is observant and takes notes to refer to. She will be a great asset to our team. The attorney is on retainer, the accountant is full time, and the seasoned sales staff is paid on a monthly basis plus commissions. They are assertive about making and finalizing sales.

With Jill onboard, I begin to travel to meet my late father's customers, sales personnel, and suppliers. Most of them are receptive. Naturally, there are a few who are standoffish and others who are skeptical. This I will work through. I have been through this in the past. After all, I am a female trying to follow in my father's footsteps. I will prove them wrong.

I am the daughter of Charles Whitford III, my father taught me well. I paid attention and made "A's" in all of his classes. After taking a month to personally meet all of the people on the list, I take a map of the United States and start drawing boundary lines. It is not an easy task. I am determined to work out the best deal for all that are involved. The customers, the sales staff, the suppliers.

With the help from my late father's attorney, we hammer out solution after solution. Who else knows my dad's business as well as his attorney? I keep some of the accounts for myself. This is what my dad wanted me to do. If not, he would have divided the business up, sold the pieces before he passed away, and gave the money to us—his children. There would not be any personal growth for me if that would have happened.

I believe my dad knew this all along and that was a part of his master plan. Some of the sales representatives do not want their own business and resign. Being a business owner is not for everyone. I admire their candor and I respect their requests. Back to the drawing board, the attorney and I redraw the boundary lines. For the people who want to keep a territory, a plan is unveiled where they can purchase the territory with all of the rights using an interest-free loan from me. In case an individual defaults the distributorship and the customers revert back to me. I am happy with this plan and I am sure dad would have been too. The new business plan is in place, executed, and working well. From time to time I refer to the journal and the letters. I find peace, security, and answers when reading them. I am always passing some tidbits on to Edward.

Chapter 29

CHARLES—HIS LEGACY LIVES ON

"Those we love remain with us for love itself lives on,
And cherished memories never fade because a loved one's gone....

Those we love can never be more than a thought apart
For as long as there is a memory, they'll live on in the heart."

Beth

Many times I have pondered and I do not have the answers to all the events that had to take place for me to meet Charles. My parents had to decide to relocate where they did. I had to choose a career in healthcare and work at the Garden of Eden. Hank and I had to meet, fall in love, get married, and not move away. Joann had to make the decisions that caused the divorce. Charles had to become ill with cancer. With not having any caregivers in the area he chose to move into assisted living which happened to be where I worked. What an amazing life we live of "cause and effect!" I remember reading a book titled "The Butterfly Effect" by Andy Andrews. The premise of the book became quite clear after meeting Charles. I was privileged to be a part of his life, a part of his dying, and how he helped me to change to live a better, more purposed life.

From his lessons, I discover forgiving another person is one of the most important things for internal peace and happiness. How I wished that I asked for his forgiveness before he passed over. I harbored in my heart for way too long the day that he screamed at me.

Making good use of the time allotted was another lesson.

Hank is learning from me and he is doing very well at his auto parts store. Hank is not a dummy and is very good with social skills. His parents taught him very well. Most of his life he was more interested in repairing bicycles, lawnmowers or cars. Growing up he did not learn how to succeed, only how to work hard. He is on the fast track now and doing very well at it. He has acquired numerous commercial accounts.

He has "House Accounts" for some of the customers that do not have the money to buy parts. I caution him about this and the possibility of losing money. His answers are always the same. "If they don't pay me that is between them and their creator. If they do pay me I will use the money to help someone else!"

Thank you, Charles!

Edward

My father knew that the most important things are unconditional love and the ability to accept a person's choice to take a different path on life's journey than tradition dictates.

Thank you dad for believing in me, allowing that to grow in me, and helping me to cultivate my God-given talents. That has allowed me to pursue a path with happiness and to develop species of plants for society to enjoy.

But most of all dad, thank you for revealing the unknown side of your life by leaving the journal and the letters. I know that

I will not help as many people as you have. I know that I cannot lighten the load for the whole world, but I can help some. I plan to cultivate the seeds you planted in my soul that are growing.

Elizabeth

I see in the mirror how much my face is glowing. There was never a doubt about his love for me.

It was the lesson of perseverance that became the foundation I built my life of success on. Most people do not achieve their dreams because they give up too soon. It stood the test of time with my family and my business.

Confucius wrote: "Our greatest glory is not in never falling, but in rising every time we fall."

Thank you dad for teaching me how to get up and that "No one ever had a Rainbow without a little rain."

Joann

The life lessons are too numerous to recall. On any given day one may be more important than any of the others.

At the top of the list, I place his never-ending love for me in spite of what I did.

He taught me that it is not important what a person's roots are. It is what that person does with their life that counts the most!

He provided for his family. He was always there for us. If he made a commitment to be with us, he kept his word even if it meant revising his schedule.

Although there is one thing that I cannot come to terms with. Charles could fix anything. Why could he not fix our broken marriage?

I love you Charles and I know you love me! Thank you, Charles! Joann.

Butch

I have to acknowledge he taught me that I am not as street smart as I think I am. Sure I am more flamboyant than he is but he got the best of me.

He is like a master chess player who lures you into his moves and suddenly announces "Checkmate" just when you think the game is getting underway. He is so skilled in the game of life.

He more than got even with me. As good as I am, I never saw it coming. Charles, you are the undisputed champion of this match. So much so I do not want it to happen again.

He came in The Majestic and never bothered a soul. He dropped a big bomb on me without a sound or any obvious actions.

He got up from his table after paying his check and left four white pills, a small mirror, and a note that said it all. The note read "Carry this mirror with you so you do not have to turn around constantly to see who is following you and what your demise is going to be."

He walked out the door and never said one word. That couple of hours with Joann has turned into many days and nights of misery. I wonder where Charles is now?

THE END

Conclusion:

In this fast-paced, very hectic world that we live in, it is easy to miss an opportunity to help someone. Almost every person you meet in life is for "A Reason, A Season, or A Lifetime!" Assistance does not always have to be money.

"A Reason" may be as simple as a smile to cheer a person up, or opening a door for someone, or assisting by picking up some dropped items.

"A Season" may be visiting a neighbor who is rehabilitation, or postponing a project to allow a bird time to hatch her eggs, or using your knowledge to mentor someone.

"A Lifetime" may be the most surprising. Such as meeting a stranger in a faraway place, Paris, France, and becoming friends for life.

During your daily activities practice being observant for ways to help make another person's day a little better. You may be surprised how simple it can be and the unspoken reward could be unimaginable!

LIFE: What are you doing with yours???

As Ralph Waldo Emerson put it, "What lies behind us and what lies before us are tiny matters compared to what lies within us."